SILVER AND SHADOW

THE FIRST BOOK OF THE DARK GODDESS

MELISSA MCSHANE

For Aerin,
your very own werewolf boyfriend

CHAPTER

ONE

Night came early in the badlands between the cities. The toothy, jagged horizon of the western mountains swallowed the sun every evening, immediately dimming its light so even the shadows disappeared. Ginnevra sometimes thought about the lands beyond the mountains to the west, whether the inhabitants of those distant kingdoms took advantage of the lingering sunlight. But then, to them it was sunrise that came slowly. Ginnevra wasn't sure she would trade the unhindered light of the morning sun for a sunset that lasted well past moonrise.

She cast her gaze on the moon she and her sister paladins rode toward. Its baleful eye had risen some hours before, and although it yet had four days to its fullest, it still loomed over them like a terrible omen. Ginnevra reflexively touched the grace she wore nestled in the hollow of her throat. The smooth surface of the black pearl reminded her that such thoughts were unworthy of the Goddess's sworn warriors. Omens implied a predestinate future, counter to everything the Dark Lady stood for, and Ginnevra needed to exercise more faith.

Her horse tossed his head at that moment as if he knew what she was thinking and scorned such fears. It wouldn't surprise Ginnevra to learn he had some insight into her thoughts, given how the paladins' mounts were bred not only to carry their heavily armored riders into combat, but to stand firm against monstrous foes an ordinary animal would flee from in terror.

She patted the horse's neck, sleek against her gloved hand. The paladins weren't encouraged to take the same mount more than twice in a row, but Ginnevra had ended up with this fellow on her last three missions, and she was as fond of him as she ever was of a horse. Secretly, she called him Stalwart, though he probably already had a name she wasn't aware of—more of the captains' desires for the paladins not to grow attached. Ginnevra wasn't a horse lover, so she didn't feel she was in any danger of that no matter what she called her mount.

Darkness amplified the sounds of horses' hooves, the jingling of tack, and the creaking of steel armor, making the small company of paladins sound like twice their number. The commonplace sounds were like music, if a strangely atonal music scored for leather and steel. The idea amused her, made her consider what other tunes plate mail might play.

A brisk breeze from the east carried the scents of the other paladins' armor and horses and a nearby river to her nose, brushing her face and neck, which were the only exposed parts of her. She turned her head to track the smell. The road the paladins followed ran through scrub plains bordered on the distant north and east by cypress trees that might indicate the river's course. From this distance, the cypresses looked like sentinel statues, tall and narrow and unmoving in the light wind. They might well have been planted on purpose to mark someone's borders, though no one rich enough to own land would settle all the way out here.

Ginnevra sniffed again, but the breeze was gone, taking the scent of water with it. Her position near the center of the double column meant she saw little beyond the next two pairs of women in line despite her enhanced vision, which had sharpened as the sun set.

She kept an eye out northward, though the barren plains gave no cover for an attacker. It was eastward she was more concerned with, the most likely approach for an enemy interested in a stealthy attack, but she had half a company between her and any potential foe, and there was no sense trying to do other people's jobs by fretting over what she couldn't see.

Beside Ginnevra, Nucca shifted her weight, making the plates of her silvered armor creak. "Is it bad that I would like something to attack us?" she said in a low voice.

"I don't think it's bad to want to destroy creatures who would kill innocent people," Ginnevra said.

"You know what I mean. We haven't seen action in three days. I'm beginning to think the reports of an ambushed caravan were wrong." Nucca let out a yawn and pushed a stray curl back beneath her padded coif. She had the most unmanageable hair Ginnevra had ever seen, even cut short to fit under a helmet as paladins usually did.

"Captain Attanante doesn't think so, and she's the most conservative thinker I know." An itch started between Ginnevra's shoulder blades, and she shrugged her shoulders to get at it. There was no way she could reach it with her hands, let alone scratch beneath the silvered steel cuirass and padded gambeson. To her Goddess-enhanced strength, her armor weighed practically nothing, but there was a limit to its flexibility.

Nucca shrugged. "It's a beautiful night, moon and all. Too bad we aren't spending it in a tavern, enjoying good ale and the attentions of attractive men."

"You're such a creature of civilization."

"Nothing wrong with that."

Ginnevra smiled. She hadn't been partnered with Nucca long, but that was long enough to have gained a sense of her sister paladin's love of material pleasures. It was true, most people would be indoors at this hour, eating and drinking and swapping tales. It was only the paladins who deliberately ventured into the badlands at night, hoping to come across and destroy the monstrous creatures who preyed on humans.

The breeze returned, stronger this time, still hinting at water and... Ginnevra sniffed. Something rank, like rotting flesh. "Do you smell that?"

Nucca came to full attention, her head tilted back. "Something dead."

Jillia, immediately ahead of Ginnevra, brought her horse to a halt, forcing Ginnevra to do the same. Jillia half-turned in the saddle. "Captain says there's something big ahead. Looks like the caravan we were sent to find."

Ginnevra looked past the paladins in the line of march, but still couldn't see anything even with her night-enhanced vision. "Nothing alive?"

"No idea." Jillia turned back to her horse and prodded it into a walk. Ginnevra nudged Stalwart forward. The smell of dead bodies was stronger now, and it heightened Ginnevra's alertness. This was the dangerous time, when their attention was focused on whatever Captain Attanante saw ahead—the time when a lurking horror somewhere else might take advantage of their distraction.

But nothing moved except the distant cypresses' branches, shifting in the slight wind. Ginnevra made herself relax the way a good warrior would, body poised to attack but not tense, eyes shifting to take in dangers, hand resting on the pistol at her hip. It was good for only one shot, but sometimes one shot was all one needed. She shrugged her shoulders and pressed her knee against the giant blade strapped to her saddle. Whatever came next, she was ready.

The columns came to a halt again. This time, Ginnevra heard the captain's high, clear voice: "Spread out, and search for survivors."

The mounted warriors broke formation, separating into pairs. With Nucca at her side, Ginnevra moved forward to see what they'd found. Her gaze took in smashed wagons, the low humps of dead oxen, scattered belongings. She automatically guided Stalwart to the right, circling the caravan, alternating between checking the wagons for survivors and scanning the plains for attackers.

She saw a body sprawled half beneath one of the wagons, but the man was definitely dead, blood covering his chest from where a club or hammer had caved it in. Another body, this one smaller, lay curled beside the dead man. Ginnevra's heart ached. She'd been a paladin of the Goddess for five years, had seen any number of atrocities and brutalities, but she'd never fully resigned herself to death.

She gazed out across the plains to give herself a moment's peace. At least this had only been a bandit attack. Bandits were awful enough, but she always felt it more deeply when it was monsters who'd killed innocents. Paladins of the Goddess were the only warriors who could effectively fight the Bright One's creatures, and it felt like a greater failure when a monster escaped her sword and gun.

Nucca came to a halt and dismounted, drawing Ginnevra's attention. "There's someone alive," Nucca said.

Ginnevra, startled, reined Stalwart in. "That's impossible. It doesn't take magical sight to know what happened here. Bandits don't leave survivors."

"I saw movement, though." Nucca approached one of the wagons, which tilted on a broken axle to form a dark, protected space beneath its bed. She moved slowly, her hand extended. "Watch my back."

Ginnevra dismounted and drew her sword, hooking the strap of the sheath over her saddle's pommel. The sword wasn't as heavy as some, only a little over four pounds, but she liked speed over brute power, and her strength combined with her lightning-fast reflexes let her wield the weapon like a blade a quarter its weight. She followed Nucca, her eyes on the wagon bed. She couldn't see in full darkness, and even the silver-blue light of the Bright One's terrible moon didn't light more than a sliver of the space.

Nucca dropped to her knees in front of the wagon bed. "It's all right," she said. "You can come out. It's all right."

Ginnevra still saw no movement. Nucca leaned farther forward. "You can—"

Something pale and thin lunged out of the darkness. Nucca gave a shriek that cut off as sharply as a knife's edge and flung herself backward. Ginnevra shouted a warning and leaped forward. Nucca lay on her back, clawing at her face with her gloved hands and thrashing as if she were trying to get away from something. But there was nothing there, not even the pale shape Ginnevra had seen. Nucca's face was red, her lips faint blue, and her hands beat at nothing.

Ginnevra dropped her sword and ran to Nucca's side. Her sister paladin's eyes bulged, and dark red scratches scored her face. Ginnevra grabbed Nucca's hands, looking desperately for her attacker. She heard voices, and heavy, rapid footsteps, and then Captain Attanante crouched beside them. "Spirit," the captain said. She wrestled with a glass bottle strapped to her hip.

Ginnevra held Nucca's hands away from her face, bearing down on her to stop her thrashing. It was like trying to hold a greased eel. Ginnevra ended up sprawled across Nucca's body, trying to weigh her down even though Nucca was heavier than she.

Finally, the captain snatched the cork from the glass bottle and upended its contents over Nucca's forehead. Salt spilled everywhere, making little piles on either side of Nucca's head and falling into her eyes and ears. Nucca choked, gagged, and lay still.

Ginnevra didn't move for a moment. It could still be a ruse on the part of the spirit. Then Nucca coughed and said weakly, "Let me up."

Ginnevra let her go and pushed herself to her knees. Nucca shook her head to rid herself of the salt, though she didn't rub her eyes. "That was stupid of me," she said.

"You should have been more careful," Captain Attanante said. "It's no surprise violent deaths like these might have bred violent spirits. We should be on our guard." She gave Nucca a hand up.

Ginnevra stood without help and retrieved her sword. Her heart rate hadn't slowed, and all her senses were heightened, ready for another attack. Nucca swayed, and Ginnevra reached for her arm to steady her. But Nucca pulled away before Ginnevra could touch her. "I'm fine," she said. Her voice was hoarse, the voice of someone who'd nearly been throttled to death.

Ginnevra examined her friend closely. Her face was dark, as if in shadow despite the moonlight, and she held herself oddly, her arms and legs limp and her head bent. "I think you should sit down," she said.

"I'm *fine*," Nucca said irritably. She drew her sword and examined its blade like she expected to find a flaw, half-turning from Ginnevra.

Captain Attanante was kneeling in front of the wagon. "There's a body here," she said. "We'll need to retrieve—"

Nucca raised her sword and swung it at the captain's back.

Faster than thought, Ginnevra put herself between the two women, bringing her sword around in a ringing block. Nucca's eyes were pure white from edge to edge, and her mouth spread in a mirthless grin. She changed position and swung at Ginnevra, a powerful two-handed blow Ginnevra only barely deflected.

The unexpected power of the attack forced Ginnevra back an incautious step. Too late, she remembered the captain kneeling behind her. She tripped and fell, just managing to keep her sword up. Nucca drove in relentlessly, her face a mask of vicious, mindless glee. From her position on the ground, Ginnevra could do nothing but block the terrible blows.

A lucky hit knocked Ginnevra's sword from her hands. Nucca raised her weapon for a final, devastating blow. Without thinking, Ginnevra snatched her pistol from her side and shot Nucca point-blank in the face.

Something shattered, sending sharp pain through Ginnevra's throat and making her gasp. Nucca's body relaxed, and her sword fell from lifeless hands, hitting the scrub ground with a muffled thud a moment before her corpse followed. Ginnevra's heart pounded hard enough to thump against her cuirass with a dull, echoing beat. The whole fight couldn't have lasted longer than the space of three breaths, and yet time continued to stretch so slowly it might as well have been honey in winter.

Someone beside her shifted. Captain Attanante got heavily to her feet and approached Nucca's body. "We'll have to bury her here, with full rites. I don't want her spirit roaming free to attack anyone else."

Her voice seemed to come from very far away. Ginnevra realized she was sitting up and someone was kneeling beside her, speaking her name. "Ginnevra. Ginna. Your throat—" It was Jillia, her hand on Ginnevra's shoulder.

Ginnevra touched her throat gingerly, and pain spiked through it. Her gloved fingers came away bloody. "My grace," she said. "What happened to it?"

"It shattered," Jillia said. She took off her glove, reached behind Ginnevra's padded coif, and unfastened the chain, then gathered the grace and chain together in her hand. Ginnevra looked at it. The black pearl in its hematite bezel had indeed shattered into half a dozen sharp-edged pieces, only some of them still clinging to its setting. Ginnevra's mind felt too numb to make sense of what she saw.

Jillia brushed at Ginnevra's throat, wiping away blood. "It's not a deep injury, just a lot of scratches."

Ginnevra nodded as if Jillia had asked for her approval. "Nucca—"

"She was possessed," Jillia said firmly. "Her soul was trapped by that spirit. You didn't kill her, you spared her further pain. Don't think like that."

"Like what?"

"Like you killed an innocent." Jillia clutched Ginnevra's hand. Her grip felt like iron bands around her fingers. "Ginnevra, it's all right."

Ginnevra nodded again. It was a lie. Nothing was all right. Nucca dead at her hand, her grace destroyed...she couldn't see that as anything but the Goddess's displeasure. And yet she felt as strong as ever, her vision was clear despite it being full night. She hadn't lost the enhancements that came with being a paladin. What that meant, she didn't know, but it had to mean something.

Then Captain Attanante was at her side. "Come with me, Cassaline," she said, hauling up on Ginnevra's arm. Ginnevra obediently followed the captain to where the horses stood waiting patiently for instructions. "Sit. We'll talk later."

"I have to help—"

The captain shook her head. Her expression was sterner than a statue's and as inflexible. "Consider yourself off duty. It's not a punishment, Cassaline. You saved my life."

That hadn't occurred to Ginnevra. She watched the captain walk away and then realized she was on the verge of collapse. So she sat beside the horses, reliving the sight of Nucca's shattered, blackened face over and over again until she heard the sound of singing. Paladins were only allowed to officiate at funerals in times of extreme exigency. This surely qualified.

They should have asked her to join them, but probably it would disrupt the funeral rites to have Nucca's killer participate. The thought sent a dull ache through her heart, as if it was already so wounded one more blow felt like nothing.

Then her sister paladins returned. None of them looked at her, and Ginnevra didn't know whether that meant they respected her pain or couldn't bear the sight of her. Again, she felt that dull ache that seemed all she was capable of.

"Cargiole, Nanciore, repair that wagon, the one to the east," Captain Attanante said. "The rest of you, load up the bodies. Cassaline, a word." She walked away without waiting for Ginnevra. Ginnevra stood and followed her.

When they were out of earshot from the others, which for paladins was a very long way, the captain stopped. She looked up at the moon and made the warding sign against the evil eye, thumb and middle finger curved to make an O, forefinger crooked above them, and the other two fingers folded in against the palm. Ginnevra mimicked her. "I don't know what to tell you, Cassaline," the captain said. "You did the right thing. Garone's spirit was already dead, and you stopped her body from committing atrocities. I know that's small comfort, because to you, it looks like you shot a friend. But you bear no blame for this."

"And yet my grace shattered," Ginnevra said. She touched the hollow of her throat, where she was so accustomed to feeling the smooth surface of the black pearl. The deep scratches had stopped bleeding, and her gloves prevented her feeling their rough surface, but the pain remained.

"And yet," Captain Attanante said. "I don't know what to make of that. It only ever happens when a paladin loses favor in the Goddess's sight. But—" She gripped Ginnevra's hand fiercely. "I do not believe you sinned against the darkness. There must be some other explanation."

"I don't know what to do." Tears rose up in Ginnevra's eyes, and she blinked them away. Crying was an unworthy reaction as well as pointless. "I can't stay with the company."

"No." The captain's lips tightened. "You'll do no one any good until you're restored. I'm sending you to Abraciabene in the morning. Someone in the holy city will know what to do."

Ginnevra nodded. At the moment, she didn't believe anyone was capable of helping her, not even the anointed of the Dark Lady. But she didn't want to argue with her captain, because how much worse would that make things? "Did you...you recovered Nucca's grace, yes?"

"We did. It was unblemished. Small comfort that her spirit now resides in the Goddess's embrace." Captain Attanante gripped her shoulder. "For what it's worth, you have my thanks. I was in no position to defend myself, the more fool me."

"It was my honor to serve," Ginnevra said, the ritual words falling automatically from her lips. Without the Goddess's magic altering her body, she would have been powerless to stop the attack, and no paladin ever accepted thanks in a way that suggested she was owed them.

The captain patted her shoulder again and gestured. "It will be a late night," she said, "but I don't want us making camp anywhere near that desolation." She led the way back to where the horses were gathered. Stalwart and Nucca's horse were harnessed to the newly repaired wagon, and Prosserra held the reins, clearly waiting for the captain's command. Ginnevra took the horse Prosserra had been riding and mounted easily. Stalwart didn't seem bothered by his demotion to cart horse. Ginnevra would have taken the change of mounts as an omen if she'd believed in omens. She didn't dare dwell on what it meant that her grace was shattered beyond repair. That might test her faith to the breaking.

She rode beside the wagon, not wanting to ride in column beside one of her sister paladins and endure any small talk the woman might feel inclined to make—or worse, ride in silence wondering what her neighbor thought of her. Prosserra was usually quiet, so Ginnevra could pretend her current silence meant nothing dire.

The night was still, with only the sounds of hooves and metal and the high whining song of insects filling the air. After a while, Ginnevra stopped hearing them. The moonlight dimmed the stars to faint pinpricks of light, which always annoyed her. On the first night of the month, when the moon was new and the Dark Lady's power at its fullest, the stars blazed paths across the sky, unhindered by any celestial light. It was tempting to think none of this would have happened at the dark of the moon, but that was foolish thinking that led nowhere good.

She tipped her head back and stared at the moon. The Bright One, the Goddess's sister who had betrayed her and all her creations. It was thanks to the Bright One that monsters existed, from the mischievous squasc to the malevolent basilisk all the way to the werewolf, that foul hybrid neither man nor beast. Ginnevra had never seen a werewolf up close, but her company had fought a pack of them once, and she had never forgotten the sense of wrongness that rose off them, stronger than their horrible musky odor.

The moon stared back at her, heartless and unfeeling as always. That was as well. Ginnevra couldn't imagine what she would do if the Bright One spoke to her. She focused her gaze on the distant horizon, where a warmer glow than moonlight marked the city of Holinne. The sight didn't reassure her. Her destiny lay elsewhere.

She had only been to the holy city of Abraciabene once before, on the occasion of her sanctification as a paladin of the Dark Lady. Now the thought of returning filled her with mingled hope and dread. Hope, that the anointed of the Goddess would have a solution for her; dread, that the solution would mean abandoning her vows, becoming outcast. Ginnevra shivered before she could stop herself having such a ridiculous reaction. Whatever her religious superiors discovered, whatever they told her to do, she would make her own path as she'd sworn five years ago. She could do no less and still retain her honor.

She hoped it was enough.

CHAPTER

TWO

T hree days later, Ginnevra rode toward the iron-banded gates
of Abraciabene, surrounded by throngs of pilgrims and traders
all intent on their business within the holy city. Abraciabene was an
ancient city, older than Ginnevra's religion, and it was ringed with
walls that showed its growth over the centuries, as if it were an oak
tree rather than one of the most dramatic structures made by
humans. Ginnevra noticed now as she had not on her first visit how
many ramshackle huts thronged the outer walls, clustering around
the road and the gate. Another century, and Abraciabene might need
another wall.

She eyed a couple of beggars holding alms-bowls by the side of
the road. They weren't doing a very good job of begging, not crying
out to the passing travelers or exaggerating their deformities—in
fact, they had all their limbs and eyes, and their extreme gauntness
was all that suggested they needed the generosity of strangers.

On a whim, she dug in her pouch and flipped a coin at each bowl.
They clinked against the few coins already there, startling both men,
who'd been looking elsewhere. "Great lady," one called out, "our
thanks, so much thanks."

Ginnevra nodded, but said nothing. She didn't actually look like a great lady at the moment, nor even like a paladin; her armor was in a sack behind her, and she wore only an ordinary traveler's jerkin over a linen shirt and plain woolen breeches, all of it travel-stained. But the enormous sword strapped to the saddle could not be disguised, and it was better than a sign for keeping away thieves and would-be attackers.

The guards at the gate examined her closely as she passed, but she judged their expressions awed rather than hostile. Unlike the beggars, they would recognize her as one of the Goddess's warriors no matter what she wore. She reflexively touched the hollow of her throat and rubbed the still-tender spot. The scratches had healed almost immediately—another blessing of the Dark Lady—but the absence of her grace made her feel exposed, as if the wound had been much deeper and left a scar.

The noise and bustle of the outer city put her on edge. Here, the thousands of pilgrims and traders mingled with the inhabitants, crowding Ginnevra despite some well-timed shoves with her boots. Everyone talked at full volume, trying to be heard over the dull roar this made, which made everything noisier. After the quiet peace of the open road, it made Ginnevra's head ache.

She forced a path away from the gate to where the crowds weren't so dense, guiding the horse northeast toward the inner city's nearest gate. This was one of Abraciabene's many markets, catering to travelers on religious business. Semi-permanent stalls offered everything from prayer stoles to obsidian trinkets for those intent on worship, while the shops beyond them offered cookware and traveling staples for men and women heading home.

Tiny obsidian mirrors hung from strings at one stall, drawing Ginnevra's eye with how they caught the light. People bought them to hang beside their doors as a symbol of the Goddess's eye watching over them. Some people believed they had magical protective powers, but Ginnevra knew better. It was unlikely an anointed had blessed the wares of a random stall owner.

The narrow cobbled streets wound randomly through the outer city. Ginnevra had heard they marked ancient cow paths, traced out by cattle until the ground wore smooth and people bowed to inevitability by paving them. She wasn't sure the story was true, but it was a good one. Tall wooden buildings lined the streets, leaving them in shadow at this time of the morning. They were tidy and well cared for, with actual glass panes in the windows and the doors hanging straight. The air smelled of wood smoke and, very faintly, of incense. The sweetish odor eased Ginnevra's headache. It was the comforting smell of faith.

The crowds thinned and quieted as she drew nearer to the second wall, away from the markets and the haggling. People made way for her on her horse as they had not near the outer gate, and she heard low-voiced comments: "...paladin..." and "...never seen one before..." and, amusingly, "...too pretty to be a warrior..." As if attractiveness had anything to do with fighting. She didn't think she was excessively pretty, with her strong features and slightly beaky nose, and her height put off many men who were shorter than she. Not like Jillia, with her rosy complexion and perfect lips, or Nucca with—

She drew in a breath as pain struck her in the middle of her chest. The horse, ignorant of her sudden distress, continued plodding toward the gate, which was fortunate because after the pain came a familiar brief numbness, as if someone had struck her a blow that radiated through all of her. She'd tried, in the three days since leaving her company, to remember Nucca as she'd been and not as the grinning, white-eyed monstrosity she'd become. And yet all she saw when she closed her eyes at night was Nucca's leering face and then the wreck Ginnevra's pistol ball had made of it.

She ground her back teeth together and forced the memory away. Dwelling on the past was unworthy of a worshipper of the Goddess. Wishing things had been otherwise implied there was only one acceptable, fixed outcome, and that was counter to the Goddess's teachings that the path mattered more than the destination. Everything she had chosen, even Nucca's actions, had led to this moment in time, and Ginnevra needed to embrace her uncertain future and trust in the Goddess's blessing.

The inner gate was narrower than the outer one, and although there were fewer people attempting entrance to the inner city, they were forced into a short queue that moved slowly past the guards. Ginnevra could technically have required everyone to move out of her way, but she'd never felt comfortable using her rank to bully people. And it wasn't as if she was in a hurry.

These guards looked even more closely at her than the others. This time, Ginnevra smiled and saluted them. Unlike the guards at the outer gate, who were under the command of the Seneschal who handled the mundane affairs of Abraciabene, these were attached to the Blessed's office and were likely anointed themselves. The two men returned her salute, looking a little stunned as if they'd experienced something miraculous.

The inner city bore little resemblance to the outer city, though both had cobblestone streets and tall, narrow buildings looming over them. Here, the streets were scrubbed clean, and the buildings were older but better maintained, with larger glass panes in the windows and flowers growing in shallow trays outside the upper windows. Ginnevra had seen other cities that looked like this, but in those cases it was the wealthy who lived there, and the inner city of Abraciabene was the residence of the anointed and those sworn to serve them.

Ginnevra quickly left the crowds behind and followed the road west. It immediately curved to the north, widening enough that an ox cart could pass and leave room for two riders. The tall, narrow buildings disappeared, giving way to stone edifices with strips of bare ground between them. These housed the paladins when they had business in the holy city. Ginnevra had stayed there during the days of her sanctification. They were even less comfortable than the buildings' exteriors suggested, but paladins were expected to endure worse than a little discomfort. She wondered if she still qualified to stay there.

The road turned again, and there was the gate to the Bastion, third ring of the city. The few people at the gate stood in little groups well separated from each other, waiting their turn. Here, the guards were clearly of the anointed, dressed in chainmail shirts over fine woolen breeches and tunics, with surcoats emblazoned with a silver-ringed black circle on a midnight blue field. Their swords, while much smaller than her own, were clearly still well-used weapons, and their faces were as stern as statues.

Ginnevra waited patiently for them to finish interrogating the small woman at the head of the line. Finally, they gestured to the woman to pass, and one of the guards looked up as if assessing the line and saw Ginnevra. His eyes widened, and he beckoned to her to join him.

Ginnevra looked at the rest of those waiting. All of them were staring at her. "I'll wait," she told the guard. "My business is not urgent, and I don't want to exercise privilege."

The guard looked skeptical, but nodded. Ginnevra watched them question the three groups in front of her, rather perfunctorily, she thought. She hadn't expected this kind of treatment. People were respectful of paladins, and frequently gave them special honors, but for the most part she didn't see any extreme displays of servility. The captains' insistence on paladins' humility made more sense now. How awful to become an arrogant, entitled woman and forget all she owed the Goddess!

After several minutes, her turn came, and she drew up even with the guards, but did not dismount. "My lady," the shorter guard said, "what is your business here?"

"I'm to speak to the Blessed on a private matter, as ordered by my captain, Biasca Attanante," Ginevra said.

"Are you expected, my lady, or should we send a runner?" the taller guard said.

"They know I'm coming, but not the time of my arrival, so I would appreciate a runner."

"Very well." The taller guard stepped through the gate and disappeared into a tiny hut to the left. Presently, a child in the same surcoat, one a little too large for her, darted out of the hut and out of sight.

The taller guard returned. "You'll need to stable your horse—no horses allowed in the Bastion, you know."

Ginnevra hadn't known, and was grateful for the warning. "At the paladins' keep?"

The taller guard nodded. "Then return, and you're free to enter without waiting again."

"My thanks," Ginnevra said, and wheeled her horse around, narrowly missing someone who'd come too close in his awe over seeing a paladin in the flesh.

The stables were to the rear of the paladins' keep, and it took very little time to hand the horse over to the ostler and arrange for her gear to be stowed, all but her sword. Feeling unexpectedly conspicuous, she hurried back to the gate and passed through with a nod for the guards.

The last time she'd been to the Citadel, she'd entered the Bastion by the eastern gate, and the northwestern one where she stood now was completely unfamiliar territory. Fortunately, it was impossible to get lost in the Bastion; it had only one main road, which was wide and paved with black basalt stones, and that road circled the Bastion with no deviation. All she had to do was walk until she reached the gate to the Citadel.

Very few people were abroad at that hour of the morning, with most of them likely at their devotions. Tonight was the full moon, which meant preparing to spend the hours of darkness indoors, away from the eye of the Bright One. Ginnevra hoped the Blessed wouldn't be so busy she couldn't see her. Now that she was here, she found herself impatient to learn what the Blessed would say about everything that had happened.

The Bastion looked like no city Ginnevra had ever seen on her travels between the city-states of the Lordagne region. Square single-story houses of basalt or black granite backed against the wall, facing smaller buildings ornamented with jet and onyx—individual shrines for worship under the dark moon. Tangled gray threads of smoke rose from narrow sticks of incense burning on every lintel, filling the air with their perfume. All the black stone made the Bastion look like a dark desert canyon, or would have if the construction of the houses and shrines weren't so beautiful. Carvings representing the Goddess and Her creations decorated the faces and lintels of the houses, soothing Ginnevra's still-troubled heart. It was impossible to feel fear or disquiet surrounded by such beauty.

The road curved visibly as Ginnevra circled the Bastion clockwise. She'd asked her first captain, back during her sanctification, whether it mattered what way you traveled the Bastion, and the woman had said, "The Goddess cares more about the meaning you give your journey than telling you what your journey means." Ginnevra had carried that piece of wisdom with her everywhere she traveled in the last five years.

The final gate, the one leading to the Citadel, faced directly north. Ginnevra knew the Citadel had once been a prince's stronghold, long before men and women worshipped the Goddess as they did now, and the gate was oriented that way because the prince's greatest enemy had been to the north. Nowadays, all that lay north of Abraciabene was the republic of Fayonne, and Fayonne's ruler, or at least the head of its council, was friendly to the holy city. Whether that had anything to do with the Blessed being his sister, Ginnevra didn't know. She remembered some of the fights she'd had with her brothers when she was young and didn't think blood kinship was a guarantee of amity.

No guards stood at the gate to the Citadel. Ginnevra walked through the short passage through the final wall alone. The corridor was dark and arched well above her head and smelled beautifully of damp stone. At the far end, the Citadel's courtyard opened up before her, a vast sweep of paving stones fitted so closely together they appeared to be a single slab into which the Citadel's bulk had been dropped.

Unlike the beautiful buildings of the Bastion, the Citadel did not look like anything dedicated to the worship of the Goddess. It looked like any of the dozens of castles Ginnevra had seen in her travels, big and stony and as solid as a mountain. Square towers loomed over the lower battlements where in an ordinary castle soldiers would have marched. Here, dark-robed and -cowled figures strolled, usually in pairs, with the occasional young messenger in the black-moon surcoat darting past and disappearing deeper into the Citadel.

Ginnevra realized she had stopped moving to stare, and now others were staring at her. None of them were paladins, for which she was grateful—and then she had to wonder why. It wasn't as if a fellow paladin could sense her disgrace, if that's what it was. But she was still grateful not to have to make small talk with one of her sisters.

She crossed the courtyard to the entrance, which was a pair of heavy oak doors banded with iron, relics of that long-ago prince's paranoia. They swung open easily, and she passed through before stopping again, this time because she didn't know where to go. She'd only ever been in the sanctification hall before, and that was an unlikely place to speak with the Blessed.

"My lady, are you summoned?"

The speaker was a short young man—Ginnevra knew nothing about children and couldn't guess his age—wearing the dark-moon surcoat and an eager expression. "I'm to speak with the Blessed," she said. Technically, she hadn't been summoned, she'd been sent, but that was none of this child's business.

"Wait here," the boy said. He ran off down the hall, which was dimly lit by torches and a relief after the bright sunlight. Ginnevra wondered why all the messengers ran everywhere, whether it was out of duty or out of love of running. No wonder they were all children, if running was expected of them. She'd never walked anywhere as a child if she could run instead.

The coolness of the hallway soon became chilly. Ginnevra rubbed her arms and settled her sword more firmly across her shoulder. Its weight comforted her, the more so because it meant she still had a paladin's supernatural strength, just like her clear vision in this dim hall meant her senses continued abnormally acute. Everything would be fine. The Blessed would explain it all, and Ginnevra could rejoin Captain Attanante's company as if nothing had happened.

She heard running footsteps before the messenger came into sight around a corner at the end of the hall. "My lady, you're to come with me," the boy said. He didn't sound even a little out of breath.

Ginnevra nodded. For a moment, she feared he would expect her to run, which she could manage, but the sword bobbed uncomfortably if she did. But he kept a normal walking pace, and she followed him easily.

The passage opened on a great hall just like ones she'd seen before, with a long fireplace and a couple of trestle tables aimed at a great dais bearing a smaller table. Stairs ascended up the sheer wall to a gallery above. The messenger led the way up the stairs and through a series of passages to another oak door the little brother of the outer door, complete with iron banding. Ginnevra just had time to wonder what made the room so special it needed extra protection when the messenger opened the door, bowing deeply, and said, "Blessed, this is the paladin."

"Enter," a woman said. Ginnevra swallowed nervously and walked through the doorway.

The room had once been a solar for the lady of the keep, Ginnevra guessed from all the big window openings on three of its four walls. But the openings had been bricked over, leaving the room in near darkness except for the many lanterns hanging where the windows had been.

The Blessed was just rising from a desk positioned between two lanterns. Fine strands of white streaked her black hair, but that was the only sign of her age; her skin was smooth, with only a few wrinkles clustered at the corners of her eyes, which were entirely black with neither white nor iris. She was paler than most women Ginnevra knew, and between that and her hair and her black robe, her face seemed for a moment to float in midair. Then she moved, and the illusion disappeared.

"I assume you are Ginnevra Cassaline," she said. Her voice was low, and she spoke with a rhythm that was almost musical. "I had a message to expect you."

Ginnevra drew her sword and saluted the Blessed the way she'd been taught to do. "I am. I hope I am not an inconvenience—I can wait, I know this is an important day—"

"For me, the day begins at moonrise, which is many hours off," the Blessed said. "Your timing is excellent. Please, have a seat."

Now that Ginnevra was actually in the presence of the holiest woman in the world, her knees shook and she was afraid to try to sheathe her sword in case it slipped and made an almighty racket on the floor. She settled for leaning it to one side with her hand gripping the hilt and sat on the footstool the Blessed indicated.

The Blessed turned her chair around to face Ginnevra and sat, slowly, her eyes never leaving Ginnevra's face. "Captain Attanante's message was quite detailed," she said, "but I believe I would like to hear the story from you."

Ginnevra swallowed again. "Yes, Holy One."

Telling the story was unexpectedly difficult, not because it forced her to relive the events of three days previous, but because she found herself resisting the urge to justify her actions. She didn't know where the desire came from, whether it was that she didn't want her religious superior to think less of her or that she wanted to lessen her guilt, but she felt deep inside it was an unworthy impulse. She had done nothing wrong, and if not for the loss of her grace, she wouldn't even be here.

When she finished the story, at the point where the paladins had made it back to Holinne with the wagon full of bodies, she discovered her hand was numb from gripping the sword hilt too tightly. She surreptitiously flexed it and rested her other hand on her knee.

The Blessed's expression hadn't changed the whole time she listened to Ginnevra speak. When Ginnevra had mentioned the destruction of her grace, the woman's hand had drifted to touch a spot just below her robe's neckline, but she'd said nothing. Now, she leaned back with her hands clasped in her lap and said, "Well. That's interesting."

Ginnevra bit back a hasty retort. "Is it?" she said instead.

"Of course. You acted appropriately, and short of revisiting everyone else's actions, which I am not inclined to do, I can't see where this calamity could have been averted."

Ginnevra made the warding sign against the evil eye without thinking and blushed when the Blessed's gaze fell on her hand. "I agree," she said quickly, "but my grace…"

The Blessed touched her chest again, then reached inside the neck of her robe and pulled out a pendant of smoothly polished jet on a silver chain. The stone was set in a hematite bezel, oval in shape, and was unexpectedly plain. The Blessed held the grace so it twisted slowly, its surface catching the lamp light now and then. "A grace is symbolic of our connection to the Dark Lady," she said. "Through it, we access Her power. Even the lowliest man or woman is entitled to an obsidian grace, and to using the small magics that remind us of Her love for us as Her creations."

She lowered her hand so the grace rested against her chest. "For those of us sworn more directly to Her service, the grace means more. Jet, for the Dark Lady's anointed, symbolic of how we are changed in our vows to Her. It wards against the influence of evil and permits the anointed to perform great workings of magic in Her name. And the black pearl, for the paladins of the Goddess." She looked directly into Ginnevra's eyes. "The black pearl is the counter to the white pearl, which is beloved of the Bright One. It symbolizes the paladin's commitment to the never-ending battle between Dark and Light."

"I thought it was what gave us our power," Ginnevra said.

"It grants the same access to small magic as any grace. Fire lighting, mending, direction finding. But a paladin's power comes from her oaths, which are binding both upon her and upon the Goddess.

So long as a paladin remains true, the Goddess grants her Her blessing. And it sounds as if that oath is still in force."

Ginnevra loosened her grip on her sword again. "I feel as strong as ever."

The Blessed sighed. "The Goddess does not direct us down a chosen path," she said, "and She does not grant us a destiny. Those things are the province of the Bright One, who would have humans enslaved to a course not of their choosing. But the Dark Lady often has lessons She wants us to learn so that we may choose more freely. I believe the Goddess has such a lesson in mind for you."

She said it so simply Ginnevra at first didn't understand. "But—what lesson?"

"If it were that simple, there would be no point." The Blessed smiled. "There is a small village some two days' journey southwest of here, on the eastern borders of the principality of Talagne. They have complained to the Principessa of Talagne about monsters threatening their town, and the Principessa, naturally, sent word to Abraciabene. I think you will be the answer to their pleas."

"You want—" Ginnevra swallowed to moisten a suddenly dry throat. "Isn't that something a company ought to handle?"

"You think you are not capable?"

Ginnevra shook her head. "No, of course not, it's just that I thought we traveled in companies as reassurance. A show of power, since we rarely kill monsters where people can see."

"That's true. But in this case, since we are talking about a small town, I think it will be better if they can put a face to their salvation. And..." The Blessed's face stilled. "It is an instinct only, but I feel this will be good for you. You need a chance to take lives that are unambiguously evil. I think it will rid you of whatever nightmares plague you."

A flash of memory struck, Nucca's blackened face, and was gone in an instant. Ginnevra swallowed again. "My lady," she said, "it will be my honor."

CHAPTER

THREE

G innevra pulled another weed, which came free of the soft earth easily. Her grip had crushed it slightly, and it let off a sharp, green scent just like any other, more desirable plant. She tossed it at the small pile of weeds and reached for another. A week ago, she would have laughed at the idea she might enjoy tending a garden. She was city born and bred, and the closest she ever came to vegetables was at the market. That was even more true when she'd become a paladin, because who had time for gardening?

But when she'd arrived at the little village of Arrus, she'd been given not a room at the inn—there was no inn, just a tavern with a couple of rooms to let—but a little cottage all to herself to the east of the village proper. And with the cottage had come the garden.

The village headman, whose name, Maghinardo, was bigger than he was, had eventually told her the cottage had belonged to one of the poor unfortunates killed by the monsters who plagued the village. He had been very reluctant to divulge this fact, and then had assured Ginnevra many times that the woman had not died in the cottage, "oh, no, not that, she was killed in the forest, so much better —not that we want anyone to die, of course!" Ginnevra had eventually taken pity on him and assured him she wasn't afraid of spooks or specters. Maghinardo had gratefully made his exit, leaving Ginnevra alone with the garden.

She'd intended to ignore it, but it was so tidy, so well cared for, she felt bad about letting it become overgrown. So she'd pulled a few weeds, just to see how it felt. Then a few more. And now tidying up the rows was a morning habit, something to do before the sun grew too hot. She liked to imagine the previous owner watching her, hopefully in approval at how well Ginnevra cared for her property.

"My lady! My lady!"

Ginnevra dusted off her hands and then her knees as she stood, squinting into the distance. The day was bright and cloudless and threatened to be very hot, but the young woman sprinting toward her across the fields seemed not to care about potential exhaustion. Nor, it seemed, did she care about the crops she was trampling. Ginnevra walked to meet her at the edge of the field and waited patiently for her to stumble to a halt, breathing heavily and unable to speak.

"Do you need a drink?" she asked. "No, don't try to speak yet, catch your breath."

The young woman, Tommasa, shook her head violently. "The well," she gasped. "Thing down the well."

Finally, a chance to do what she'd come for. "Wait here," Ginnevra said, and strode off to the cottage. She dragged her chain-mail shirt over her head, tugging her short hair free where it caught on the links, and gathered up her sword. No time for the full kit, but then she likely wouldn't need it. Thing down the well, huh? It might be nothing—after all, this wasn't a new village, and what were the odds something had only just moved in, or come to light after a century of peace?—but she couldn't take a chance on that.

Tommasa barely waited for her to emerge before dashing away. Ginnevra jogged after her. The mail shirt wasn't much of a weight, and she could run for miles without being winded, but she liked to assess her surroundings before diving in head first.

Arrus, as the Blessed had said, wasn't a very big village. It was mostly a collection of cottages about the size of her own on the road eastward from Talagne, with a respectably-sized tavern the only thing setting it apart from dozens of other little villages on the frontier. That wasn't entirely true. It was also, unusually, quite a ways from any other settlement, and its farmers were used to wild animals encroaching on their property. The appearance of monsters was more recent.

It seemed most of the village had gathered at the town square, where the community well was. There were enough people Ginnevra couldn't see what lay past them. She pushed gently through the crowd, which parted for her as soon as they realized who she was, and approached the well.

It looked perfectly innocent sitting there in the morning light, its gray stones slicked with water around its mouth. The rope wound around the windlass was frayed into a single dangling length, the bucket missing. Ginnevra held her sword to one side and scanned the small clearing. Nothing but frightened villagers.

"What happened?" she asked.

No one spoke at first. Then the headman's wife, Piatta, said, "Olavena was drawing water when the bucket stuck. It wouldn't come up no matter what she did. Then there was a snarl, and the rope snapped. We all heard the snarl, my lady. No question."

"All right. Stand back." It was an unnecessary warning, as it looked like no one had any intention of getting close. Ginnevra approached the well, listening. She heard the movement of water, deep below—or was it something else? The smell of fresh water had a hint of bitterness to it, like soot.

At the lip of the well, she stopped and listened again. This time, she heard breathing, light and rapid and not very far away. She fingered the frayed end of the rope. It was slightly damp, but had snapped as if it had dried in the sun for a week. Something had pulled on it, hard.

Cautiously, she moved closer until she could barely see down the well shaft. She had no desire to make herself a target, silhouetted against the sky for whatever creature was down there to attack. The bitter smell was stronger now, a dark thread against the coolness of the water.

She saw the bucket, bobbing gently at the bottom of the well, a dark blotch against dark water. It looked deformed, warped out of true—and then she made out the outlines of a creature clinging to the bucket. It had oversized ears like a hare's, but fatter and more sharply pointed, that stuck out from its round head on both sides, and its back was arched as if it was trying to keep as much of itself away from the bucket as possible. Small fingers and toes gripped the wood tightly, shifting to find a better hold.

A moment's sympathy touched Ginnevra's heart. The creature looked frightened, trapped in a place it didn't understand. Then it tilted its head back, and its eyes met hers. They were sheer white, the only light thing about it, and focused fiercely on her. It snarled, made a leap from the bucket to cling to the wall, and scurried up the irregular stones, headed for her.

Ginnevra stepped back and raised her sword. "Back away," she told the crowd, which hastily took several steps back, though none of them fled. Ginnevra ground her teeth in frustration. She wouldn't let the creature get away, but suppose something went wrong, and it attacked one of the villagers? People were so stupid sometimes.

The scrabbling of sharp nails on stone grew louder, along with the rapid breathing. Ginnevra shifted her weight for a firmer stance. The noises stopped. There was a moment of perfect stillness during which Ginnevra didn't relax her pose or her grip on her sword. She heard the movement of the crowd and shouted, "I said, stay back!"

The monster shot out of the well like something had flung it. It grabbed the dangling end of the rope and hung there for a moment, its head jerking as it looked in every direction.

"Over here!" Ginnevra shouted.

Its blank, white-eyed stare focused on her. It shrieked, a high-pitched, challenging sound. Then it leaped from the rope, pushing off the windlass, and hurtled right at Ginnevra.

Ginnevra brought her enormous sword around in a great sweep that sang through the air, a clean and beautiful tone that contrasted wonderfully with the monster's shriek. It caught the monster at its midsection and kept going, slicing it in half as easily as cutting fruit. The creature let out another shriek, this one agonized, and then its bisected body landed at Ginnevra's feet, its hot black blood steaming even in the warm morning air.

Ginnevra held her position for a moment longer, letting the tension bleed out of her. Then she bent to wipe her blade on the short grass. The grass sizzled and darkened wherever the monster's blood touched it. She then poked the pieces of the body with the sword's tip, though it was clearly dead.

"No, stay away," she said as the crowd moved in for a closer look. "It's a squasc. Their blood can burn flesh. Somebody see if they can retrieve the well's bucket, and I'll need water and a wooden box."

She squatted back on her heels as the crowd dispersed slightly. The bitter smell had vanished when the squasc died, which surprised her, but she was too grateful for its absence to wonder about it. Fur covered its body, longer on its head and around its feet, and it looked much less dangerous in full daylight than it had in the well. It had already begun to sag in death, its features sinking in to give it a hollow look. Its eyes, still stark white, bulged in comparison, like a couple of soft-boiled eggs.

Maghinardo himself brought her a box and stood nearby as she gingerly picked up the squasc's pieces and dropped them inside. "Is it safe to use the well?" he asked.

"Perfectly safe. Though not if this creature had bled into it. I'm glad it was willing to be taunted."

Maghinardo touched his chest, where his grace lay beneath his shirt. "Thank the Goddess you were here."

"It was my honor to serve." She accepted a bucket of water from one of the villagers and poured it over the remaining smears of black blood. Another hiss arose, and a thread of steam, but both were barely noticeable. "You should burn this patch of grass. The water will keep the blood from hurting anyone, but nothing will grow here until the blood is removed."

"Of course." Maghinardo tugged on the cord around his neck, pulling out his grace, which was a flat chunk of obsidian with a hole drilled through it for the leather thong. He crouched beside the still-steaming grass and said, in a low but clear voice, "*By Your grace I wield the fire.*"

A spark kindled on the grass and quickly spread, ignoring the water still clinging to some of the blades. As if it knew the extent of the squasc's blood, the blue-tinged fire spread only as far as the contamination, and after a short time, it burned itself out, leaving an ashy residue. Maghinardo stood and dusted off his hands as if he'd touched the fire's remains. "You have our thanks, my lady."

"It was my honor to serve," Ginnevra repeated. She poured more water down the sword's blade, just in case; the corrosion didn't harm metal, but she didn't want to touch any of it by accident.

Accompanied by Damiano, the village blacksmith, she carried the box well away from the houses in the direction of the forest. Damiano was a cheery, powerfully built man with curly brown hair and arms like sides of beef, and he carried a couple of shovels as easily as if they weighed nothing. "I guess we've all gotten used to no more monsters," he said. "That was a scare and no mistake."

"Squasc are really only dangerous because of their blood. I'm sure you all could have handled it otherwise." Ginnevra set down the box and accepted a shovel.

"Still, we're glad you're here. Nothing like a paladin to fright the monsters away!" Damiano grinned.

They dug a hole in silence, for which Ginnevra was grateful. She liked Damiano—liked almost all the villagers she'd had contact with —but she felt the weariness that always came after the excitement of fighting a monster, even one as easily killed as the squasc. It was an emotional rather than physical weariness, and one that passed after an hour of peace and quiet.

When the hole was finished, she lowered the box into the ground and helped Damiano bury it. "It won't poison the earth, will it, my lady?" Damiano asked.

"The blood's corrosive influence breaks down a few days after the squasc dies." Ginnevra tamped down the dirt over the hole with the flat of the shovel. "By the time the wood rots, the remains will be harmless. This is just an extra precaution."

"You'd know best, I warrant," Damiano said. "I'll carry that, my lady."

Ginnevra handed over the shovel. "Thanks for the help."

"It's no trouble." Damiano rested the two shovels on his shoulder, but didn't head back to the village. "Do you think the monster trouble is done?"

Ginnevra cast a glance at the forest. The road that passed through Arrus narrowed the closer it got to the forest until it was hardly more than a trail. "I don't know. I patrol the edges of the forest every day, but I haven't gone much deeper because that's dangerous with there only being one of me. Safer for everyone if I watch for anything willing to brave the village. But I wonder if I need to take a closer look."

"You should take care, my lady," Damiano said in alarm. "Suppose there's something stronger than even you can handle? It might not be safe."

"It might be more unsafe for me not to pursue the threat more directly." Ginnevra turned and walked away. "But I don't take unnecessary risks. It really does look like the threat has died down."

Damiano followed her. "I hope you're right," he said as they parted company, him to return to the smithy, her to go to her cottage.

Back at her cottage, she wiped the blade off with a scrap of cloth, then drew on her new grace, nestled in the hollow of her throat, to burn the cloth. "*By Your grace I wield the fire,*" she said, pronouncing each word of the prayer deliberately. Before losing her old grace, she had been, as most paladins were, almost careless about her invocations. The Goddess never seemed to mind if you weren't paying full attention to what you said, and invocations were so common it was easy to say them all in a rush. But now that Ginnevra knew what it felt like to be without the Goddess's grace, she made her observances in a more deliberate fashion.

As the final word of the invocation left her lips, a spark of flame kindled in the end of the cloth Ginnevra held from her fingertips. The fire quickly spread, turning blue-green where it burned the squasc's blood, until its heat seared her fingertips and she had to drop what was left of the cloth on the hard ground outside her front door. When the fire burned itself out, she ground the few remaining ashes into the earth, then kicked a little loose dirt over the spot and tamped it down with her foot.

She removed the mail shirt and wrapped it in its oiled cloth before putting it away, then carefully examined the sword one last time before sheathing it and standing it in the corner. Her cottage was just two rooms, a place for sleeping and a place for eating, but neither of those rooms looked like they belonged to an ordinary cottager, with her weapons prominently displayed in the front room and her plate mail armor arranged in the sleeping room like a second guest. She checked the finish of her plate mail even though she hadn't used it. Hadn't needed it at all since coming to Arrus. The thought was bittersweet.

She returned to the garden, but after the excitement of killing the monster, the thought of pulling more weeds lost its appeal. Well, there weren't many left, and they would keep until morning. Instead, she sat on the bench in its sliver of shade next to the front door, stretched her long legs out, and tilted her head back. With her eyes closed, all the sounds felt within reach of her hand: the cries of birds in the forests some quarter mile away; the wind swooshing through the barely-grown crops; the slight creaking of the shutters Ginnevra kept meaning to fix. Even the very faint sound of children chasing each other around the cottages was intelligible. The children never came this far out, which was probably for the best, but when they weren't more than a sound, Ginnevra enjoyed their presence.

Seven days in Arrus, and the squasc was the first real threat she'd faced. Not that it had been much of a threat, but it would likely have hurt someone if she hadn't been there. Even so, she'd started to feel she was here under false pretenses, or at least for no real reason. The villagers all had stories to tell about monsters preying on Arrus, and Ginnevra had no reason to think them liars, but none had attacked the village until today.

Just this morning she'd been thinking it was time to leave. The Blessed hadn't said how Ginnevra was to know when she'd learned whatever it was the Goddess had in mind for her, and Ginnevra had begun to wonder if her skills wouldn't be better used elsewhere. Somewhere actually under threat of destruction. But whenever she considered leaving, fear struck her. Not fear of the future, which would be ridiculous, or fear of monsters, which was even more so. She couldn't put a name to this fear, and that was what kept her in Arrus—the desire to understand why she was afraid of leaving.

The sun's shifting rays obliterated the narrow stripe of shadow she'd sat in. She got up and stretched. She'd run through her training regimen before dawn, had pulled weeds until midmorning, had slain a squasc before noon, and now she would eat and then walk her patrol route. Far from being bored, Ginnevra enjoyed her routine. Paladins were taught to look for opportunities to learn in the most tedious of situations, and Ginnevra believed boredom was just another word for laziness.

She carved a hunk of cheese off the quarter-wheel by the fireplace and cut herself two slices of thick, nutty bread bought from one of the villagers. Getting them to accept payment had been difficult, and she'd almost let them press food on her for free. But that was the fast way to become entitled and selfish, and paladins existed to serve. The bread was delicious, heavy and rich with seeds and bits of nut and slightly sweet with honey. The cheese, smooth-textured but with an unexpected bite, complemented it perfectly. She washed her meal down with fresh water and a handful of pitted olives, then retrieved her chainmail and her sword and headed for the forest.

It was hard not to see her patrol of the forest as a pleasure walk, despite being armed and armored. The great oaks with their spreading leafy canopies provided welcome shade against the afternoon sun—and it wasn't even summer yet, Ginnevra reflected as she walked the tree line. In the distance, Arrus went peacefully about its business, the farmers tending their crops, the householders tending their cottages, the children still screaming in whatever game they were playing. It was the kind of day where believing in monsters seemed impossible.

Ginnevra's feet in their sturdy boots crunched fallen twigs and dry grasses underneath. She moved as quietly as she could, not for fear of being heard by animals or monsters, but so she could hear animals or monsters approach. That was unlikely, given that most monsters preferred the cover of night, but she might get lucky.

Ahead, she saw a squirrel scamper up a tree trunk and paused to give it time to get away. That was the kind of animal she liked to see, the kind that wouldn't attack her or require her to kill it. And squirrels were cute, with their bushy tails and alert, inquisitive faces and skittering movements. Squirrels, and voles, and foxes, and even wolves—those, she liked. Though it was unlikely there were wolves anywhere within a hundred miles of this place. They didn't like humans any more than humans liked them.

She paced the tree line a mile away from Arrus, then turned around and walked another mile and a half in the other direction. Nothing stirred. She didn't see so much as a flash of fur or a twitch of a tail. Arrus was as safe as she could make it.

She headed back to her cottage, thinking hard. The people of Arrus had had a serious complaint, or the Principessa wouldn't have sent for help from Abraciabene. And yet she hadn't seen monsters to justify her presence in a full week of living there. Despite the answer she'd given Damiano, she didn't think the trouble was over. It was unlikely the monsters had gotten wind of her presence and stayed away, because most monsters weren't intelligent, and the intelligent ones, the malignae and werewolves and lamias, would just have altered their hunting patterns. So something else was going on, but what?

She put her armor and sword away and washed up. Some nights, she visited the tavern for supper, but tonight she didn't feel like having company. Particularly since there was a good chance the villagers would feel compelled to shower her with praise for killing the squasc. Praise from her fellows was one thing; praise from people who already considered her their superior was uncomfortable.

She lit a fire in the hearth and filled the pot with water before cutting up vegetables for soup. It was one of the few foods she could reliably cook indoors, and she wasn't in the mood for hunting, skinning, and cooking rabbits on a spit.

She paused with her knife held above the cutting board. Not in the mood for company, not in the mood for cooking that required effort. She should be careful not to talk herself out of absolutely everything on the grounds that she "wasn't in the mood." Tonight was the half-moon, with the world poised exactly between dark and light, and maybe her restlessness was related. She resumed chopping. The half-moon was an invitation to take action, to champion darkness against light. Time for her to take a more aggressive stand.

She swept chunks of vegetables into the pot, which hadn't yet started to boil, but uncharacteristic impatience had taken hold of her. She'd been cautious long enough, and the villagers had almost paid for it. If that monster had been more dangerous than a squasc, someone might have died. She needed more information. So what if there was only one of her? She should hunt the forest after dark. Maybe the monsters' behavior would become clear.

CHAPTER
FOUR

Just after sunset, she once more donned her chainmail and hefted her sword. Her plate mail was more complete protection, and it comforted her to wear it, but for this, she wanted the flexibility and relative silence of chainmail. Before leaving, she checked that her other weapons were ready and in good shape. She propped the loaded arquebus outside the front door, its match unlit. She'd used it only a couple of times, against crows that had tried to pick her garden clean, but although it was old and slow to reload, she felt about it the way she felt about her pistol: sometimes one shot was all it took.

The pistol, too, was loaded, but not with shot. Ginnevra carried a little sack with gunpowder in twists and a handful of silver musket balls sized to fit the pistol. The fact that she hadn't seen any evidence of werewolves didn't deter her from taking precautions. Like the arquebus, she would be grateful for the silver ammunition and the silvered armor and blade if they were ever necessary.

The moon wouldn't rise until well after midnight, which cheered Ginnevra. The moon's light would benefit no monsters tonight.

Sword sheathed over her shoulder, she crossed her small yard and headed for the forest.

She loved this time, the hour after the sun's disc slipped fully behind the distant mountains and left a peach-colored glow behind, fading to dusky deep blue. The sky was as clear and cloudless as it had been all day, and stars scattered across the midnight blue canopy like specks of shattered glass. Ginnevra breathed in the cool evening air and scented the greenness of the crops growing in their fields behind her and the water in the distant well and a dozen smells of people's suppers. She let her breath out slowly, unwilling to disturb the evening's calm with even so small a noise as her breathing. It almost convinced her to give up on her hunt, sit by the garden and listen to the night noises of owls and people moving around in their houses and a billion insects singing just at the edge of perception. But she had a duty.

The noise of people, audible only to her enhanced hearing, faded as she neared the forest, and the sounds of night birds grew louder. Experience told her the birds would stop singing when she was near them, but that applied to any possible predator, and she intended to use the birds as a warning. The insects continued chirruping no matter what she did. Eventually, she would simply stop hearing them.

The forest rose up like a wall before her, dark and filled with moving shadows as the upper branches shifted in the light wind. Dodging a low-hanging branch, Ginnevra ventured into its depths. Very little grew on the ground beneath the dense canopies, and her footing was secure, so she felt comfortable not watching her feet as she moved farther in.

She left the fields behind only a dozen paces in, the trees closing in around her like thick velvet curtains. When she turned, she couldn't see her cottage. Brushing her grace with her fingertips, she murmured, *"By Your grace I come home."* A warm spot like a tiny flame kindled within her chest, tugging to her left. North. There was a larger magic that drew a person back to a location rather than marking true north, but that was the province of the anointed. And this little magic was enough for her. She let her sense of north sink into her bones, then continued walking eastward.

The birds left off singing every so often as she passed beneath their trees. She heard nothing to indicate she wasn't the only person in the woods. Idly, she tried to remember what night had looked like before she was a paladin. Shades of gray, she thought. Certainly nothing like what she saw now, the trees sharp-edged blackness rising to dusty green leaves, the few bushes and weeds dark green against the lighter ground, everything as clear as day, just darker. Ginnevra found it comforting.

The deeper she traveled into the forest, however, the more unsettled she became. She ought to be disturbing the nocturnal animals who lived here, but she saw nothing, just as she had on her patrol that afternoon. The birds became fewer, and quieter, until there was nothing but the sound of the blood thrumming in her ears and her feet treading near-silently across the ground.

She became aware she wasn't alone just as she smelled it: a rank, sweet-sour odor like rotting flesh, but with musky overtones that told her this was no decomposing deer or skunk. Ginnevra stilled, listening. Still nothing. Then, faintly, a scraping sound—the sound of a foot dragging across the forest floor.

Ginnevra listened for another footstep. There, to the left. She moved lightly in that direction, careful to avoid the undergrowth and lifting and placing each foot precisely to keep from making the same noise her prey had. Silently, she sniffed the air. The rank, musky odor was stronger, and she felt she'd smelled it before. Surely something that noxious would be instantly memorable?

She froze as the creature moved again, this time away from her. No wind moved beneath the branches, so she had no idea whether it had scented her, but if it knew she was there, it intended to avoid her. And if it didn't...well, there was no sense trying to read the creature's mind. She could kill it just as easily if it didn't know about her presence.

A whiff of the same scent reached her just as she took another step, freezing her in place again. The same scent, but without the rank decomposing odor. She took a breath to still her suddenly racing heart. There were two of them. And now she recognized the scent.

Werewolves.

A shiver ran through her, not of fear but of superstition. She sternly told her imagination to be still. Thinking of werewolves earlier hadn't conjured them up. Now the forest's unusual stillness made sense. Animals feared werewolves even more than humans did, and no monster would encroach on a werewolf's hunting ground. And if there were two of them...no, if a werewolf pack was in the area, she would have noticed it. These might be at the limits of their territory—or worse, scouting the area to expand their territory.

Ginnevra's feet kept moving as she mulled over possibilities in her mind. She couldn't allow the werewolves to prey on the village, or to take word to the pack that here was good hunting. But, *two* werewolves? She'd never fought one alone, just as part of a paladin company against a pack. She was sure she could kill a werewolf, but she wasn't so arrogant as to think it would be an easy victory. Two of them, she wasn't as sure. But her mind kept straying back to her memories of Arrus, peaceful and defenseless in the sunlight. She had to try, for the villagers' sake if not her own.

She listened, and sniffed the air again. She couldn't keep down-wind of the creatures, not here beneath the trees where the wind didn't blow, but she could hear their movements and work her way around to a better position. Then she would draw one of them away for the kill.

The first werewolf, the one who stank worse than the other, was still headed north and west. For a moment, Ginnevra considered letting it go. It would almost certainly come out of the woods far north of Arrus. But that meant leaving it free to attack some other settlement, and that was unacceptable.

Quietly, she reversed course and retreated westward, then

followed the stinky werewolf north. The unnaturally silent forest rose up around her as she slipped between the trees, still avoiding the underbrush. Her prey wasn't trying to be stealthy, which made it even more likely she'd be able to sneak up on it. Whiffs of its odor came to her nose occasionally. She couldn't smell the other one anymore, which worried her. That probably meant it was too far away to be a problem, but she hated not knowing her enemy's location.

Movement ahead made her pause in the shelter of a large oak. The creature was lower to the ground than a human and moved with a smooth grace that revolted Ginnevra, as if it was a natural animal and not an abomination. It was black and difficult to see clearly, but still obviously much bigger than an ordinary wolf. It continued to trot at a leisurely pace, showing no sign it was aware of her presence.

Ginnevra waited for it to gain a little distance on her before following again. She mentally reviewed what she knew about killing werewolves. Silver wasn't as deadly to them as the stories claimed; it made fatal certain blows a werewolf would otherwise shrug off, and it was slow poison if it entered their bodies and stayed there, as with a ball or a dart. But cutting off a werewolf's head was as final as it would be to any creature, and doing enough damage even with a non-silvered weapon could kill it too. Ginnevra wasn't sure how much "enough" was, but it didn't matter; she had silver, and skill, and that would have to do.

She risked getting a little closer for a better look. In its wolf form, the werewolf's shoulders were about chest-high on her. She'd never seen a lone werewolf close enough to tell if this one was bigger than average. Too bad she couldn't trick it into assuming its human form, which she'd been taught was easier to kill, but werewolves knew this too. This one wouldn't give up any advantage.

The werewolf abruptly stopped, and Ginnevra stopped half a heartbeat later, fear and excitement thrilling through her. It lifted its head as if scenting the air for enemies. Ginnevra resisted the urge to draw her sword, which would definitely be audible. She put her hand on her pistol, which she'd taught herself to shoot with her off hand, and waited.

The werewolf stood still for another very long moment. Then, with a gesture that was almost a shrug, it continued on its way. Ginnevra relaxed. Careful not to disturb the undergrowth, she followed, one hand on her sword. Almost time to lure it in a direction of her choosing.

In the next moment, faster than thought, the werewolf turned and lunged for her.

Startled, Ginnevra tried to draw her sword and her gun at the same time and confused herself enough to draw neither. The werewolf gathered its powerful hind legs beneath it and launched itself at her throat. Ginnevra threw herself backward, out of reach of its snapping jaws, and yanked her pistol free of its case. She aimed at its midsection and fired.

The creature was damned fast, faster than anything its size should be, and despite the nearly point-blank distance between her and it, the werewolf impossibly dodged. Not entirely—it yelped as the ball struck, not its unprotected stomach, but its left flank. It kept coming as if she hadn't hit it at all.

Ginnevra dropped her pistol and scrambled to her feet, then had to throw herself to one side to avoid the werewolf's claws and viciously sharp teeth. She reached for her sword again, but hadn't even gotten a hand on it before the werewolf was on her again. This time, its claws struck her chainmail, and it howled as if burned. Despite herself, Ginnevra grinned. She was no helpless villager.

The trees grew too thickly for much evasive movement, but Ginnevra didn't want to evade, she wanted to kill. She darted left and finally managed to draw her sword, flinging the sheath at the werewolf, who dodged. Now she and the werewolf circled each other, teeth bared, looking for an opening. Ginnevra's instincts took over, years of training and fighting guiding her hand. The werewolf's stench was almost overpowering at this distance, but she ignored it, all her attention focused on her moving feet and steady hand on the sword and the creature's huge paws padding between the trees.

Her foot came down on an exposed root, making her stumble, though not enough to bring her down. The werewolf, seeing an opening, lunged for her. She brought her sword up between them, angled to impale, and the creature once more dodged so her blade slipped along its rank, matted fur without penetrating its hide. Ginnevra screamed as its jaws came down on her shoulder, grinding the links of the chainmail into her flesh.

The werewolf's howl of pain was louder than hers. Ginnevra smelled singed fur, as if contact with the silvered metal had burned the monster. Then its weight bore her to the ground, pinning her chest and upper arms.

Ginnevra swung wildly, but the angle was all wrong. Snarling, she got her feet between them and *shoved* with all her strength. The werewolf rolled to one side, recovering its balance instantly. Without hesitation, it rushed her again. Ginnevra realized it was going low instead of high too late to do more than swing hard at its neck, a blow that made the wolf stagger, but didn't stop it.

Hot, tearing agony shot through her left leg, which suddenly wouldn't support her. Ginnevra fell, and the werewolf followed her, aiming its powerful jaws at her unprotected, bloody thigh. She thrust with her sword, and this time she connected solidly with its shoulder, making it howl again. She hitched herself and her useless leg backward until she came up against a tree she could put her back to. Then she rose on her right knee, tucking her left leg under her, and assumed a guard position, breathing heavily enough to send shudders through her body.

The werewolf halted some distance away. It started limping back and forth, its terrible golden-brown eyes never leaving her face. Ginnevra's hand shook, and she steadied herself with her left hand pressed against the blood-soaked earth. Everything was growing dark, as if someone had shrouded the trees in black veils. Her leg hurt so badly it took all her concentration not to fall over. Still the werewolf didn't advance. Small comfort that it was injured, too—she was clearly worse off than it.

"Come on!" she shouted, pointing her sword at its heart. "You cowardly vermin-ridden monster, come on and see if you can take me!" Her sword weighed so much. She didn't remember it being this heavy before. Dread weighed her down as heavily as the sword. Werewolves weren't stupid. It was just waiting for her to weaken, and then it would attack. She had to get up and go on the offensive, bad leg or no.

Shuddering, she pushed herself to one foot, keeping her sword steady. The reek of werewolf made her want to vomit, it was so strong. Her left leg wasn't responding at all. She screamed mentally at herself—*get up, you weakling, don't let this scratch stop you*—but nothing helped.

Her sword hand trembled again, and the tip of her blade sagged. The werewolf stopped pacing and sprang. Ginnevra tried to lift her sword to the ready, but now her hand wasn't obeying either. Time slowed as it sometimes did in battle, and the werewolf seemed to float in midair, slowly but inexorably drawing nearer. In a haze of pain, she wondered how much it hurt to be torn apart by a werewolf.

The werewolf was inches from her face, its stinking breath hot and wet on her skin, when something struck it from the side, knocking it away. Ginnevra blinked, but the world had gone gray, and all she could hear was the werewolf snarling, and heavy bodies colliding. She couldn't tell if she was still holding her sword. Then she was lying on the dead leaves covering the forest floor, breathing in the smell of decomposition. So much nicer than werewolf stink.

The snarling echoed, making the werewolf sound like two werewolves, and added to that was the roar of the ocean in her ears, almost drowning out the snarls. Ginnevra closed her eyes and listened to the ocean until it faded away, and unconsciousness claimed her.

CHAPTER
FIVE

S he came to herself out of a strange dream in which she was wrapped in a wolf's skin and rolled down a hill with no bottom, bouncing and jolting uncomfortably but not painfully. Gradually, she became aware of her surroundings—firelit wattle and daub walls, the smell of burning logs, her body resting on something neither hard nor soft. Something covered her, a blanket or cloak or something, and she was uncomfortably warm. The ceiling was too far away—no, she lay on the floor of a cottage, not on a bed. *Her* cottage, she realized.

With that, memory washed over her. She grunted and tried to sit up. Pain spiked through her leg and shoulder so sharply she nearly vomited, and a gray mist rose up over her eyes. Blinking away tears, she lay still again and closed her eyes.

She heard footsteps, and a shape moved between her and the fire, blocking its heat. Ginnevra's eyes shot open. At first, the person was nothing but a black blob against the firelight, but after a moment, the black blob resolved into a large man leaning over the hearth to lay on a few more logs. Ginnevra moistened her lips, which were parched from the fire. "I think it's hot enough."

The man turned to look down at her. He was no one she recognized, definitely not one of the villagers. From her perspective on the floor, he looked to be about eight feet tall, which was almost certainly not true. His hair and short beard were dark, and there was something wrong with his eyes Ginnevra couldn't identify with his body backlit by the fire. His clothes, smudged as if they hadn't been washed in a few days, didn't fit him very well; the shirt strained across his shoulders, and the trousers were too short. Looking at him made Ginnevra feel uncomfortable, as if she had invaded his privacy just by observing what was visible to anyone.

"If you want," the man said, setting aside the second log and retrieving the first before it could catch fire. His voice was deep and resonant, and it made her disquiet grow, though she didn't know why.

Ginnevra tried once more to sit, more cautiously this time. Her right shoulder where the werewolf had bitten her burned as if all the muscles were torn, but she managed to prop herself on her left elbow. "Who are you? Did you bring me here?" It was a ridiculous question, because whoever he was, farmer or woodcutter or traveler, there was no way he could have defeated the werewolf that had tried to kill her.

The man didn't say anything. He walked over to her table and pulled out the one stool, seating himself as if he was weary. From this perspective, his proportions made more sense. He wasn't eight feet tall, but he was almost certainly taller than she was. She had rarely seen men his size before. It didn't matter, because he still couldn't—come to think on it, how *had* she survived the attack? Something had struck the werewolf, but a paladin wouldn't have come to her rescue and not stayed to make sure she was well.

She leaned more heavily on her elbow and reached beneath the blanket, her own blanket from her own bed, to prod at her leg. That hurt, too, but not as badly. Someone had cut away her ruined breeches and hose and bandaged her leg, expertly if her fingers were any guide. Ginnevra's gaze shot to the still figure seated at the table. "Did you do this? Who *are* you?"

The man hooked one heel over the lower rung of the stool. "My name is Eodan," he said.

"That's nice, but it doesn't tell me anything. How did I get here? What happened to the werewolf?" Too late, she realized he might be scared of werewolves, and casual mention of them might make him flee. She didn't want him to flee. She wanted him to explain himself.

Eodan shifted his weight. "The werewolf is dead," he said, as casually as if he was talking about a dead sparrow rather than a monster.

"But—" Ginnevra drew in a breath to batter him with more questions, and stopped, her heart in her throat. The smell of burning wood had overridden other smells, but that deep inhalation had brought more of them to her nose, the smell of cold candle wax and the pungency of cheese and the clear, clean scent of water in the bucket—and a horrible, all too familiar musk. The fresh, very near odor of a werewolf.

She shot upright, fear overriding pain, and shoved backwards until she ran up against the wall, knocking over the pile of wood by the hearth and the mace propped in the corner. Never taking her eyes off the stranger, she fumbled the mace with nerveless fingers until she got a good grip on it and brandished it at him. "What are you?"

Eodan looked at her with no sign of fear. She probably looked harmless, between her wound and her terror, but let him attack her and he would see how harmless she was. She was very aware that the mace wasn't silvered because it didn't have an edge, and the odds of Eodan holding still while she beat him to death were not good. It was still a better weapon than nothing at all.

The silence stretched out between them. Finally, Eodan said, "I'm the person who saved your life."

"The *hell* you are," Ginnevra shot back. But she couldn't help thinking how strange it all was. Someone had killed the werewolf— the *other* werewolf, she corrected herself—and brought her home and bandaged her wound. But it couldn't possibly be this...this *creature*. And yet why would someone else do all that and leave?

Eodan scratched his head with one enormous hand. "I'd been following Colc—the werewolf you fought—for several days, looking for a chance to attack him. I didn't realize you were even there until I came upon the fight. I stopped Colc killing you, and then I bandaged your leg and brought you here."

"How did you know this was my house?" Ginnevra's questions were multiplying like rabbits in spring. She clung to this question, feeling if a werewolf knew where she lived, she was in more danger than all of Arrus.

Eodan shrugged. "Your scent is all over this place. I took a chance."

The reminder that no matter what he looked like, this creature was not human, jolted Ginnevra out of her stupor. "Get out," she said. "Get out before I kill you."

The corner of Eodan's mouth rose briefly, enraging Ginnevra further. But he only said, "You're not in any condition to care for yourself. You're lucky Colc didn't sever an artery, that's how bad your wound is. You need help."

"Then I'll find someone else. Someone human. Get out of here."

Eodan stood and walked to the water bucket. He filled one of the wooden cups on the shelf above and brought it to Ginnevra. "You look parched. I'm sorry I built up the fire so high, but it's important to keep warm when you've been seriously wounded."

Ginnevra almost struck the cup out of his hand. She didn't want a werewolf's help, certainly not one who wanted Goddess knew what from her. But she was suddenly very thirsty. She took the cup and drank down its contents, not looking at Eodan. Eodan, for his part, stood from where he'd crouched next to her and returned to sitting on the stool. Now that he wasn't backlit, Ginnevra could see his eyes clearly. They were blue, not a color she'd ever seen before. She would have imagined him blind if he couldn't obviously see.

"What do you want from me?" she asked. She realized she'd set the mace down when she had her drink, and closed her hand over its haft without raising it. She had to admit she was weak enough that there was nothing she could do to defend against Eodan if he chose to attack her.

Eodan spread his hands wide, a gesture indicating harmlessness —as if Ginnevra believed that. "I wanted you to live. It's my fault Colc made it this far, so it's my fault he attacked you."

"I don't believe you. You could have left me in the woods, or left me here in the cottage, and I would never have known you existed. Do you know what I am?"

Eodan was silent again for a moment. "We call you hunters in darkness," he finally said. "The sworn warriors of the Dark Lady. I don't know what you call yourselves."

"It doesn't matter. I kill your kind. As soon as I'm well, I'm coming after you. So you'd better get a good head start." Absolutely none of this made sense. Werewolves didn't kill their own kind, they didn't save humans from their own kind, and they certainly didn't care for injured humans so they wouldn't die. And yet Eodan—the creature had a name, like he was a person!—had done all those things. Ginnevra held onto her bold words, hoping she could make them come true even as she felt in her heart she couldn't kill someone who'd saved her life, even a monster. What kind of paladin did that make her?

Dizziness struck her, and suddenly her arm wouldn't support her. She sagged, then fell over, hitting her head on the floor. Clammy sweat broke out on her forehead and upper lip. Her chest ached as if she couldn't draw a deep enough breath to reach her lungs. "The water," she managed through thick lips. "You put something in the water."

"Your wound is contaminated," Eodan said. He was kneeling beside her, or at least there was a man-sized dark blur looming over her, but he sounded as if he was speaking from the bedroom. "Colc's claws. It's the werewolf nature fighting your humanity."

Ginnevra closed her eyes because Eodan's dark bulk made her even dizzier. "Turn me...into..."

"No. That's a myth, that a werewolf's bite or claws turn humans into werewolves. It's far more likely to kill you." He sounded so matter of fact Ginnevra almost didn't understand his meaning.

"Then...leave me," she said. Her tongue was as swollen as her lips, and she had to work to force the words out. "Let me...die...you unnatural...bastard."

"I can't do that." Again, he sounded as if they were discussing the weather, not her life. "I cleaned the wound as best I could, and I'll clean it again as soon as the water boils. But you hunters are strong, stronger than most humans. I think you'll live through this."

He sounded even farther away than before. Ginnevra licked her dry, cracked lips. She said, "Then I don't...need you...survived worse..."

She heard Eodan talking over her, words that now made no sense, and she wasn't sure she'd spoken aloud. Her body was too heavy to move. The blanket drifted away, leaving her exposed to the merciless fire, and then she felt nothing.

When she woke again, she lay in her bed, and it was morning—late morning, by the slant of the sun's rays. Her head was clear, and she remembered everything that had happened the night before, if it was only last night. She might have slept Goddess knew how long.

She lay still, listening, but no sound indicated anyone else was in the cottage. Her light, easy breathing was all she heard, with not even the music of the birds or the raucous croak of crows come back to denude her garden. She was alone.

Grimacing, she tried to sit up. Her shoulder no longer burned with pain; it felt more like she'd strained those muscles with the way they ached. Her leg, too, had stopped feeling as if it had been torn off, though she didn't think it would support her. It took her two tries to get to a sitting position, and she was sweating and dizzy when she succeeded. When the world settled, she gingerly rotated her right shoulder. It felt stiff, again as if she'd suffered a bad strain, but the more she moved it, the looser it became.

The cottage door opened and shut, sending a thrill of fear through her. She cast about for a weapon, but saw only her plate mail armor. There was no way she could don it in time for it to protect her. Without thinking, she swung her legs around to stand, and the pain in her thigh spiked just enough to stop her putting weight on it.

The bedroom door swung open, and Eodan entered. He didn't look surprised to see her awake and sitting. Ginnevra couldn't remember ever seeing emotion on his face. She glared at him to conceal the fear she felt at being unarmed and unarmored, defenseless against his attack.

"You do heal fast," Eodan said. "I thought you would be unconscious for another day beyond this, after the worst passed." He came fully into the room, but didn't shut the door. In daylight, he didn't look quite as imposing as he had beside the fire, but he was still a good five inches taller than she, judging by the door frame, and his shoulders and arms were massive. The blue eyes looked even stranger in full light.

Ginnevra struggled with herself, fighting the knowledge that she shouldn't make polite conversation with a monster, and lost. "How long have I been out?"

"This is the second day since you were injured," Eodan said. "Can you stand?"

She hated admitting to weakness before him. Again, she lost the battle. "No."

"I'll bring you something to eat." Eodan turned and left, again not shutting the door.

Ginnevra squeezed her eyes shut and cursed herself. She had a duty to kill him, and never mind her current physical condition.

Werewolves were the Bright One's most powerful creation, made to mock the Goddess's human children. They were vicious and cruel and killed without mercy.

And yet.

She didn't understand Eodan's game. He'd saved her life, treated her wounds, and hadn't attacked her when she was too weak to fight back. For a vicious monster, he was doing a damn good job pretending to be civilized, with his quiet, contained movements and his refusal to be baited by her threats. And he'd killed one of his own kind for her sake. Werewolves never did that. They were devoted to their kin and protected them against every attack.

She'd fought werewolves before. She had seen their true nature. Eodan must want something from her to behave this way. Ginnevra didn't want to think about what it meant that a werewolf was smart enough to know how to lull a human into complacency. An ordinary human, of course. No paladin would let herself be fooled by such a ruse.

Eodan came back holding a tray. It held sliced cheese, half a loaf of bread, also sliced, and a basket of pears as well as a cup of water. Ginnevra's stomach revolted at the sight of so much food. "I don't feel very hungry," she said before remembering she didn't want to give away any of her weaknesses.

"I didn't know which way your appetite would go," Eodan said. "I've never known a human to survive a werewolf attack. Eat what you want. The rest will keep."

His casual admission reminded Ginnevra what she was dealing with. "Never stayed around to watch your victims' fates?" she snapped.

For the first time, his control wavered as his lips tightened like he was holding back an angry answer. "Think what you like," he said. He set the tray on the end of the bed and retreated to the doorway, but didn't leave the room.

Ginnevra stacked a thick slice of cheese on a thicker slice of bread and took a bite. The bread was warm from the oven, and fear stabbed her heart again. "Where did you get the bread?" she demanded.

Eodan's calm returned. "From the village."

Ginnevra sucked in an outraged breath and coughed when a morsel of cheese went down the wrong way. "You *dared*," she said when she could finally speak. "You keep away from them, do you hear? Keep away from them, or so help me I will tear you apart."

"I didn't hurt anyone. I even paid for it." Astonishingly, he smiled, an expression that lightened his face. "They believe I'm your brother, come to tend you in your illness. No one's asked the obvious question of how I knew you were sick to come to your aid."

Ginnevra realized she'd crushed the dense bread in her anger. She opened her hand and let the fragments fall onto her blanket-covered lap. "I don't want you here," she said. "I can care for myself."

Eodan's smile vanished. "You don't remember the worst of your illness. You nearly killed yourself by bashing your head against the hearth when you had fits. I wasn't going to abandon you just because you have some irrational fears about my kind."

"It's not fear," Ginnevra snapped, "and it's not irrational. I've fought werewolves. I know what *your kind* are like." He had to be lying, part of his plan to get her to trust him.

"You know what you're taught," Eodan said. "Are you done eating? You should see if you can sleep some more."

Ginnevra picked chunks of bread from her lap and crammed them into her mouth. She still wasn't very hungry, but she needed food if she wanted to regain her strength. "That's all I want," she said around her mouthful.

Eodan picked up the tray and left the room. Ginnevra shook the crumbs from her blanket, but didn't lie down. She knew she was being stupid. She did want sleep, but she didn't want to give the werewolf the satisfaction of being right. A tiny bit of guilt gnawed at her. If he'd protected her—no, it was impossible. She hadn't just been told about werewolves, and her knowledge didn't come from unsubstantiated rumor; she'd seen them attack with her own eyes.

She knew what they were like. Eodan was trying to trick her. She wished she knew why.

Her eyes ached with tiredness. Sighing, she lay down and pulled the blanket to her chin, though it was a little too warm for this late spring day. As she drifted off to sleep, she resolved to get the truth out of him. Maybe then she could figure out what to do.

CHAPTER
SIX

It was another two days before Ginnevra could walk unsupported. Eodan never offered to help her and she didn't ask. Instead, she'd exercised her leg as best she could from her bed until it no longer hurt as much. Then she'd practiced standing with her hands on the bed for balance, holding her position until she shook too much to stay upright. She'd gone on practicing until finally, on the second day, she hobbled from her bed to the bench by the front door and collapsed onto it, breathing heavily. The air was warm and smelled of the nearby fields and, closer to hand, fresh pears.

She realized Eodan stood beside her with the basket, and she took a pear without thinking about how it might look, whether he might think she was softening toward him. The trouble was, he was just so damned *patient*. He never responded to her taunts, never threatened her, never raised his voice. He responded to her every word as if they were having a civil discussion, which was rarely true. And the more patient he acted, the worse Ginnevra felt.

It was because he looked human, she decided. Nothing about him shouted "werewolf" except perhaps his scent, and she'd gotten so used to his presence she barely noticed it anymore. Yes, he was bigger than most men, and he had those peculiar eyes, but in general, he looked human. And Ginnevra would never treat a human as rudely as she did Eodan. Hence her inappropriate guilt.

She reminded herself every night that he was a monster, someone she was duty bound to protect humans from. The words had started to sound hollow. She'd never known a monster to act against its nature. They weren't mindless; they had instincts that let them judge how dangerous a human opponent was, and Ginnevra had known monsters to flee rather than engage with the enemy. But those were a monster's only reactions, fight or flight. They never showed compassion for a wounded enemy, and they never pretended to be harmless and friendly.

And Eodan hadn't behaved at all like the monster he was. Even the possibility that he was doing all this to trick her into doing what he wanted seemed less plausible the more time passed. No werewolf should be able to behave like a human, even in pretense. It was far more reasonable for him to kill her than to put on an elaborate show to influence her actions.

Which all made Ginnevra increasingly convinced she didn't have the full story.

She bit into her pear, which was underripe and a bit too hard but still juicy, and listened to Eodan eating his own pear without looking at him. She wished she knew what he was thinking, not right that moment but in general. She wanted to know what had motivated him to save her life. Whether it really was altruism as he'd said, or whether he'd seen an opportunity to put a paladin in his debt. She couldn't imagine why a werewolf would think that necessary.

"Why did you do it?" she asked, impulsively.

Eodan didn't answer immediately. "Why do you care?" he finally said.

His answer surprised Ginnevra. It was the closest he'd ever come to striking out verbally. "Because it makes no sense. We're enemies —worse than enemies, because I am a paladin sworn to kill your kind. You should have let me die and spared your people whatever death I might bring upon them. But you didn't."

Eodan again was silent for a moment. Then he wound up and threw the last of his pear far away, past the garden and into the fields bordering on the forest. "I don't know. I told you I felt responsible because Colc wouldn't have been there for you to fight if I hadn't chased him so far west, but you're right that you are my people's enemy. All I know is that I couldn't have lived with myself if I'd let an injured person die. Even a human hunter."

For the first time, curiosity rather than anger touched her heart. "Why were you chasing him?"

Eodan bit into another pear. Ginnevra thought he might be giving himself time to come up with an answer. "I didn't want him telling the pack where I was," he said.

That raised all manner of secondary questions. Ginnevra went with, "Why would that matter?"

"Don't worry about it. It doesn't concern you."

His voice, normally so placid, had gone hard and cold, and Ginnevra felt a pang as if he'd lashed out at her instead. She didn't like the feeling, as if he mattered to her at all, so to counter it, she said, "Some kind of feud, then? I didn't think werewolves had feuds. Or are you outcast?"

To her surprise, he let out a mirthless *hah* of laughter, one short, sharp sound like hands clapping. "Something like that. You don't really care, do you?"

That sounded like he really meant *I don't want you to care.* Perversely, Ginnevra pushed harder. "I'm curious. You're the one who's always saying I don't know anything about werewolves—don't you want to take the opportunity to educate me?"

For a moment, Eodan didn't say anything. Then he hurled the pear's core to follow the first. "It's not as if you'll believe me."

She was surprised again, this time that he sounded so bitter, as if her not believing him mattered. "Try me," she said, and for once felt she'd been honest with him.

Eodan took a seat on the bench, as far from her as he could get. Guilt and embarrassment struck Ginnevra again, because it was the gesture of someone who knew he was unwelcome and didn't want to intrude. Well, he *was* unwelcome. She meant that thought as defiance, but it sounded weak and childish in her head.

"We're not all in agreement, the werewolf packs," Eodan began. "Most of us want to live in peace, as far as that's possible, with humans. You don't bother us, we don't bother you. But some werewolves still owe allegiance to the Bright Goddess—"

"Wait," Ginnevra said, impulsively laying a hand on Eodan's arm to stop him. "What do you mean, still? You are the Bright One's creatures."

Eodan looked at where her hand rested on his arm. Ginnevra blushed and snatched it away, too fast for politeness. But Eodan didn't look offended. "I told you you wouldn't believe me. You're convinced you know the whole truth and you're willing to kill for that truth's sake. Things are far more complicated than you believe."

He sounded just as he always did, not angry or vehement but calm, and something shifted in Ginnevra's head. He was a monster. He was who she was sworn to fight. And he'd saved her life twice over and had never once done or said anything to injure her. She didn't care anymore that it was madness to trust him in any way; she believed he was telling the truth. "I'm sorry," she said.

It was Eodan's turn to flinch. For once, he looked perfectly astonished. "Sorry for what?"

Ginnevra looked full into those odd blue eyes. "I've killed werewolves," she said, "and I'm not sorry for that, because they would have killed me. But I knew you were different almost from the start, and I'm sorry I didn't listen to my instincts. From what I've seen of you, I can believe your people aren't all of a kind. And I want to know the truth."

Eodan blinked. He said, "Even if you don't like what you hear?"

"I'm a paladin. We face the hard truths so others don't have to," Ginnevra said.

The corners of Eodan's mouth quirked up, just for a moment. "I believe it." He let out a breath and said, "Most of us would rather not come to the attention of our Goddess. We have a history—but that's not important to this story. What matters is that some of us still serve Her, and that number has grown in recent years. About seven moons ago, my pack was torn by strife over whether we should commit ourselves to the Bright Goddess. Those in favor of doing so won, and those of us who disagreed were either killed or fled. I fled."

Ginnevra recalled what else he'd said. "Your pack hunts north of here. Your former pack."

Eodan nodded. "I didn't stray too far. I searched for others who'd become outcast, hoping to take them to safety with an allied pack. I didn't find many, but enough...anyway, Colc stumbled on me while he was on long patrol, and was returning to the pack to let them know where I was. I had to kill him before he could report in."

"And then I blundered in." She realized she was still holding an uneaten pear and took another bite. "Blundered in, and nearly got myself killed."

"You nearly killed Colc. He was lucky to have wounded you so severely, because he wouldn't have survived many more of your attacks." Eodan leaned forward with his elbows on his knees. The position made his shirt strain even farther against his broad shoulders.

"I didn't think I'd done much damage." Ginnevra recalled how the pistol ball had almost missed, how none of her blows with the sword had seemed to do more than glance off the werewolf's hide. "I think you're flattering me."

Eodan smiled, his eyes lighting with amusement. "I don't know how it looked to you, but Colc was fading from the silver in his wounds. They left him weak to my attacks, and between that and his exhaustion from trying to outrun me, I killed him easily."

"Then...you're welcome, I suppose."

They sat in peaceful silence for a while, eating pears and flinging the cores with their bitter seeds across the garden. Ginnevra stretched out her still-sore leg. Eodan glanced at it. "You really do heal fast."

"We do. It's one of the gifts the Dark Lady bestows on Her paladins. Physical strength, acute senses, excellent reflexes, toughness and healing...this wound couldn't have been inflicted by anything but a werewolf, or maybe a maligna or a marabbecca. Nothing else is strong enough." She wondered idly if she should be telling him these things, because suppose she was wrong, and he was an enemy who would use them against her? But she still couldn't bring herself to believe it.

Something else struck her. "How did you get my chainmail off if silver is so deadly to you?"

"It wasn't easy," Eodan said with a grimace. He idly rubbed one hand against his trouser leg. "I wrapped my hands in cloth and moved as quickly as possible."

Ginnevra's gaze focused on his hand. The inside curve between his thumb and forefinger was red, redder than rubbing would make it. She grabbed his hand and forced the fingers open. "You didn't say anything about being injured."

Eodan gently removed his hand from hers. "It isn't much, and it's mostly healed now. Besides, it's my own damn fault for handling silvered mail."

"Still—" More guilt surged, guilt and a discomfort she didn't have a name for. "Thank you. For saving my life."

Eodan laughed, startling her so much it was like an electric jolt. She had never even imagined him laughing. "I didn't expect thanks. Not from you."

"Why, because I'm stubborn and angry and convinced you're evil?" Ginnevra shot back, more harshly than she'd intended. She wasn't sure if he'd been laughing at her, and it hurt more than she would have guessed.

The laughter stopped. "Because you don't like feeling helpless," Eodan said, "and you don't believe anyone deserves thanks for embarrassing you."

His insight made her feel uncomfortable again. "I'm not so arrogant I won't acknowledge when I owe a debt," she said.

"No," Eodan said. "Not that. And I didn't do it to be thanked."

Ginnevra nodded. "When we are thanked, we say—the paladins say—it is our honor to serve. We do what we do because we are blessed by the Goddess, and not because we are strong or capable of ourselves."

"Interesting," Eodan said. "And yet you'd have to be strong to start with, wouldn't you, to even think of becoming a paladin. How is that not false modesty?"

Ginnevra rose and limped around to Eodan's end of the bench. She braced herself, took hold of the bench with one hand, and lifted that end and Eodan so his feet left the ground. He grabbed hold of the seat to steady himself, and he looked so astonished she would have laughed if she'd had any breath to spare. She was still too weak to hold it very long, and she was shaking when she set it down again, but she was reassured to know she hadn't lost all her strength to her injury.

"There," she gasped, and limped back to her seat. "No ordinary human woman could manage that. The fact that I can is entirely due to my Goddess. It's why only women are paladins—that's the Goddess's sign to humanity that She has power, because otherwise women are almost all weaker than men. But it's not so much that we think less of ourselves, or that we're unworthy, just that we acknowledge where our abilities come from. We're encouraged not to think of ourselves as deserving of praise...oh, I'm saying this badly."

"You mean you don't want to take undeserved glory," Eodan said. "Because that might have other humans thinking you're what they should worship."

"That's it exactly." Ginnevra leaned back, relishing the warmth of the sun that soaked into the walls of the house and then into her. "So, if you don't worship the Bright One, what do you worship?"

Eodan turned his head so she couldn't see his face. "Nothing," he said. "We have turned our back on the light, and the darkness doesn't want us."

He sounded so bleak Ginnevra regretted her idle question. "I'm sorry I asked."

"It doesn't matter." He still wouldn't look her way.

Ginnevra stretched out her leg again. "I'm not much for theology," she said. That made him turn and look at her, eyebrows arched in disbelief, and she laughed somewhat self-consciously. "I know, it sounds strange, a paladin not caring about religion, but the truth is most of us live our lives on the edge of civilization, and theology— the high, abstract questions about good and evil and the nature of divinity—there's no use for that there. We know the Dark Lady loves us, and we know She grants us Her power, and that's more than enough."

Her leg ached, and she tried a different position, gingerly rubbing the edges of the healing wound through the bandage. "So maybe my opinion doesn't mean anything, but I can't believe it doesn't matter that you're outcast from your Goddess. Or—I don't know. It's increasingly clear everything I thought I knew about werewolves is suspect."

Eodan smiled slightly. "Whereas everything I thought I knew about hunters in darkness turned out to be true. Bigoted, aggressively hostile—"

He was teasing her. The world was upside down. She scowled at him to conceal her amusement. "And you saved my life anyway. Doesn't that make you a traitor to your own kind?"

His smile fell away. "Maybe," he said. "I'd like to think it means I am open to learning the truth. And those who follow the Bright Goddess will say I'm already a traitor for turning my back on Her. I suppose I might as well be damned for following my conscience as for betraying my faith."

"So why did you?" Ginnevra asked. "I realize I'm biased because I believe the Bright One is evil, so I think it's good you chose not to obey her, but I'm not sure why one of those who are the pinnacle of her creation would feel that way."

Eodan set the basket of pears, mostly empty now, on the ground. He leaned against the cottage wall and laced his fingers together in his lap. "We have stories of our creation. Probably they're not the same ones you tell, but that's not important. What matters is that when war came between the Bright Goddess and the Dark Lady, most werewolves wanted to stay aloof from the conflict. The tale is that werewolves were peaceful people who sorrowed at how creation was divided into Light and Dark, and we didn't like the idea of fighting a battle that wasn't technically ours. We thought the argument between the two powers should be sorted out by them."

"You're right, that's not the story we tell. Sorry. Go on."

Eodan closed his eyes. "But the Bright Goddess had other plans. She and the Dark Lady fought through the proxies of their creations: humans on one side, monsters on the other. And when werewolves refused to fight, she overrode our free will and forced us into battle." He smiled bitterly. "She claimed it was our destiny."

"But that's awful," Ginnevra exclaimed. "No wonder you wouldn't worship her. That any Goddess could do that to Her creations—that's *appalling*."

Eodan opened one blue eye and looked at her. "I don't need your pity."

"This isn't about pity, it's—Eodan, how is that fair at all? You reject an evil Goddess, but the Dark Lady won't accept you because you're not Hers—you shouldn't be left alone in the world." Ginnevra's hand clenched into a fist. "Though it seems like there *is* something we're taught that's true—that the Bright One takes away all your choices but the one that leads you back to her. I wish for your sake that weren't true."

Eodan sat up. "I take it back," he said. "You're nothing like what I believed a hunter would be."

Ginnevra blushed. "I defend humanity against monsters," she said. "I just didn't know everything that meant." She stood and hobbled to the doorway, grabbing hold of the frame to support herself. "I think I need to lie down for a bit."

"I'm going into the village for a couple of chickens to stew for supper," Eodan said.

"What," Ginnevra teased, "you're not going to hunt them?"

"Feathers stick in my throat," Eodan said, perfectly straight-faced.

At sunset, they ate stewed chicken, rich with gravy they mopped up with more of the nutty brown bread. Neither spoke, but this time it was a companionable silence, not strained and silently hostile the way previous meals had been. Ginnevra could almost forget Eodan wasn't human. He had perfect table manners, which made Ginnevra wonder what werewolf society was like. But she felt awkward asking the question, as if it would break their amity by reminding them both of their differences.

Instead, she said, "Eodan, if most werewolves are like you, shouldn't we humans know about it?"

Eodan glanced at her. "That was abrupt. Have you been thinking about it long?"

"I guess so. I just think, if you're not evil, shouldn't that be public knowledge?"

"Because convincing you I was harmless was so easy, you mean?" Eodan smiled that bitter smile again. "Imagine trying to convince, say, those villagers to trust intelligent wolves that outweigh them. They know even less about monsters than you do."

"True, but I was thinking of the Blessed—she's the leader of our Faith, and she ought to know the truth."

Eodan shrugged. "Tell her if you want. She won't believe you."

Ginnevra reflexively brushed the grace at her throat. "Or you could tell her."

Eodan's eyes widened. "Me? You're out of your mind."

"You're very convincing. And maybe there's something she can do."

"Something she can do? Like, petition the Dark Goddess to welcome the outcasts into Her fold?" He sounded more sarcastic than she'd ever heard him.

Ginnevra felt uncomfortable at his reaction, but she persisted. "I don't know. I don't think you should be punished for turning your back on the Bright One, doing something all humans are blessed for, just because you're a..." She refrained from saying the word *monster*.

"We don't need charity. And we don't care what humans think of us." Eodan put down his fork and pushed his bowl away. "Don't think you have to go to any trouble."

Stung, Ginnevra said, "Don't you have children? Should they have to suffer—"

"It's none of your business," Eodan said. "Leave it alone, Ginnevra."

Ginnevra forked up a large piece of chicken and stuffed it into her mouth. Stupid, arrogant, self-centered—well, if he wasn't willing to listen, the Bright One take him. It wasn't as if they were friends. She didn't care what happened to him or his people.

Someone banged on the door, and a voice shouted, "My lady! We're under attack!"

Ginnevra cursed and shoved back from the table, knocking over the stool Eodan had borrowed from someone in the village. She limped to the door and flung it open. A woman stood there, tears in her eyes. "What is it?" Ginnevra said.

"Oh, my lady, it came out of the forest, all dark but with white eyes, and we stood against it because we know as how you're not well, but it tore Stefano apart and drank his blood. Everyone ran, and they're mostly indoors now, but it's flying around and shrieking like nothing I've heard before. Please, my lady, we need help!"

"Get inside," Ginnevra said, though she heard nothing—and then, from the village, a high-pitched cackle, a sound that ran down her spine and touched a primitive fear she suppressed. "Maligna," she said to Eodan. "I need my armor."

"You're in no condition to fight," Eodan said.

"Neither are the villagers, and I have to do something." Ginnevra hurried to the bedroom and shook out her chainmail like it was linen, freeing it from its wrappings.

Eodan followed her and shut the door behind him. "You're going to be killed."

"That's not a given. And if I am, it's how all paladins want to go—"

He grabbed her unwounded shoulder. "This isn't funny. Just wait until dawn. A maligna can't open doors, and it will batter at those houses until sunrise and then fly away. No one has to be hurt."

Ginnevra firmly removed his hand from her shoulder. "You really don't know anything about paladins, do you?" She pulled the chainmail over her head, casting a glance at the plate armor nearby. Someday she'd have enough notice of a disaster to be able to use it.

"Then I'm coming with you," Eodan said.

"Excuse me?"

"Or do you think I'm not capable?" Eodan stood with his arms crossed over his chest. He looked powerful, someone who could hold his own in a fight, but Ginnevra's heart sank.

"It's not that," she said. "This isn't your fight."

"No, but I'm not about to watch you go into danger and get wounded again after all the trouble I went to to save you. Didn't you say malignae were as tough as werewolves when it comes to attacking paladins?"

He looked so determined Ginnevra couldn't bear it. "You can't fight in that form," she said, lowering her voice so the villager couldn't hear them. "It's too vulnerable. Malignae have claws and teeth worse than a werewolf's."

"Then I'll change. It's not as if anyone will see me, locked inside their houses as they are." Eodan looked grim. "You don't make my decisions for me, Ginnevra."

"Fine," Ginnevra said, and threw the bedroom door open. She didn't have time to argue. In her heart, she was grateful not to face the monster alone, but it felt so strange knowing she would go into battle alongside a creature she'd sworn to kill.

She snatched up her mace from beside the fireplace—a maligna's hide was strong enough to resist edged weapons, but nothing resisted having its skull staved in by a three pound spiked lead ball. "Stay here," she told the woman, who was visibly shaking. "Sit by the fire and try to calm down. We'll be back soon."

The woman eyed Eodan, who with his broad chest and well-muscled arms looked more dangerous than Ginnevra felt she did. "Good luck, you and your brother," she said.

The arquebus still stood propped against the door frame. Ginnevra snatched it up one-handed and muttered *"By Your grace I wield the fire"* almost too rapidly to be intelligible. The Goddess would understand. The end of the long cord that was the arquebus's match glowed. Ginnevra couldn't remember what she'd loaded it with, but she hoped it was something that could hurt a maligna.

Ginnevra and Eodan hurried across the fields as fast as Ginnevra's healing leg could manage. Every step sent a flash of pain through her, but pain was nothing. She could endure those little pains forever. Eodan clearly wanted to outpace her, which with his longer legs would be possible even if she hadn't been wounded, but kept close to her side.

The shrieks of the maligna grew louder as they neared the village. Eodan stopped abruptly. "Keep going," he said. "I have to change." He removed his shirt and kicked off his shoes.

"Why—oh." Ginnevra's assumptions embarrassed her. Of course

a werewolf's clothes wouldn't transform with him. She turned her back on him and kept going.

It was only a few moments later she sensed him approaching, padding along on nearly silent paws, the werewolf musk stronger than it was when he was in human form. "Malignae have hard hides," she told him, trying not to feel odd about talking to what looked like an animal as if it was a person. "Your claws likely can't hurt it unless you go for the throat. They're strong and fast and they look too heavy to fly on their skinny little wings. The best approach is to get it on the ground."

She gestured with the hand holding the arquebus. "I'll use this first, see if I can't anger it enough to come down to attack. Once I shoot, watch for your moment." She grinned. Her vision had sharpened as the sun set, giving the night a clarity different from that of daylight. The moon was waning toward full dark, and she felt alive, her whole body humming with the best kind of tension, the kind that heightened all her senses and readied her to attack.

Eodan nodded, an absurd gesture on a wolf the size of a small bear. His eyes, Ginnevra noticed, were as blue as ever. Ginnevra nodded back and crept forward, hunched slightly, her eyes and ears alert for danger.

The shriek of the maligna came out of nowhere, very close to hand. Ginnevra identified the house it had come from and circled around its neighbor, trying to get a look. The air smelled of wood smoke and supper and the foul scent of the maligna, a mixture of dead earth and rotting vegetation that sickened Ginnevra. She'd fought malignae before, though never alone—but she wasn't totally alone, was she? She hoped Eodan wouldn't get in her way. He might be strong and a fighter, but he couldn't be a trained warrior, and novices sometimes were more trouble than they were worth.

The house the maligna was attacking lay on the main road through the village, such as it was. Ginnevra peered around the front corner of its neighbor, looking up at the roof of the single-story cottage. The maligna clung to the rooftop, tearing at the thatched roof and shrieking in rage at not having a target of flesh instead of the thatch. Its skinny wings, batlike except for being translucent, flapped slowly, keeping it in position. Its mouth with its many needle-like teeth and its chest were covered in dark red blood. Eyes that were solid white from edge to edge showed no sign of where it was looking.

Ginnevra set down her mace and quietly hefted the arquebus in both hands. Moving slowly, she stepped out from cover, hoping she was right that the maligna was too furious to notice anything not immediately in front of it. She aimed the heavy, bulky weapon and pulled the trigger.

The explosion nearly deafened her, and she jerked as the arquebus leapt in her hands. Above, the maligna's shriek became one of pain. It fluttered away from the roof, looking around for its enemy. Ginnevra tossed the arquebus aside and snatched up the mace. "Down here, bastard," she shouted. "Come and get me!"

The maligna shrieked again and dove. Ginnevra was ready for it. Leaning on her uninjured leg for support, she swung the heavy mace with both hands, putting her whole weight into the blow.

The mace connected with the maligna's left shoulder, a good solid hit that knocked the maligna sideways to collide with the nearest cottage. Ginnevra followed, but her leg slowed her enough that the maligna was in the air again before she could take another swing. But Ginnevra had heard bone crack, and the thing's left arm hung limp. It was an encouraging start.

She decided not to chase it, which would be pointless given her wounded leg. Instead, she put her back to the cottage and raised the mace threateningly. "You come down here and we'll see what you've got," she taunted, though malignae weren't intelligent enough to understand more than a few basic human words.

The maligna darted back and forth like an indecisive bee, then with another shriek dove at Ginnevra's face. The reek of decomposition sickened Ginnevra, but she readied her weapon and swung. The maligna pulled up short, and Ginnevra's blow struck only air. It overbalanced her, and by the time she regained her balance, the maligna was at roof level again.

Ginnevra smacked the haft of the mace against her other palm. Her left leg was on fire with pain, her right leg ached from having to bear all her weight, but she felt good despite all that, strong and capable and ready to smash skulls. In passing, she wondered where Eodan was, but didn't let the thought distract her. That was the sort of thing that could get her killed.

The maligna dove again, its right claws extended and its bloody teeth bared. Ginnevra waited this time, refusing to be caught by the same trick twice. She swung, and connected with the creature's midsection, but not as solidly as she wanted. The blow knocked the maligna aside enough that its claws barely grazed Ginnevra's armored shoulder. Ginnevra immediately pressed the attack, slamming her mace at the thing's head.

It dodged with a snarl, doubled back, and threw itself at Ginnevra's face. Ginnevra incautiously dodged left and collapsed as her leg gave out. She swung the mace again, but the hit glanced off the maligna's tough hide without doing more than slow it down.

A large, dark shape flew past, leaping over Ginnevra as she sprawled on the ground and taking the maligna around its armored middle. Eodan rolled, carrying the maligna with him, both of them clawing and kicking and biting like a couple of animals. Ginnevra pushed to her feet and limped after them, mace at the ready. The two were so entangled she hesitated, not wanting to hit Eodan.

Then Eodan got his powerful hind legs between them and shoved the maligna away to fall gracelessly on its back, its horrible wings splayed out beneath it. In an instant, Eodan was on the monster, pinning its shoulders and going in for the kill. Blood spurted, and Eodan raised his muzzle and howled. The maligna convulsed, then lay limp and bloody beneath the werewolf.

Ginnevra grabbed Eodan's shoulder without thinking and didn't recoil when he turned on her, snarling, his shoulders heaving with exertion. "Shut up," she hissed. "Do you want everyone to know you're here?"

Eodan took a step back, away from the maligna's corpse. Then he turned and ran.

Ginnevra watched him go until the cottage door opened and a man stuck his head out. "Was that a wolf?" he asked. Then he saw the bloody body and made the warding sign against the evil eye. "Praise the Goddess, you killed it!"

Ginnevra hoped no one here knew enough about fighting to question how her mace had bloodily ripped out something's throat. "It's dead," she said. "Was anyone hurt? Anyone else, I mean? I heard it killed Stefano."

"A few people got clawed before they could reach safety, but Stefano was the only death." The village headman, Maghinardo, hurried toward her. "Thank you. Are you hurt? You look injured."

"It's an older wound, nothing to worry about." Ginnevra tried to pick up the maligna's body and realized she couldn't manage that and her mace and the arquebus, certainly not on an injured leg. "You'll need to bury it somewhere well away from the village—sorry I can't do that, but—"

"No, no, you've done more than enough," Maghinardo said. "Please, go rest. We'll handle this. Should we be worried about the wolf? I heard it howl."

"That was just the maligna's death cry," Ginnevra lied.

Maghinardo didn't look convinced, but he said nothing more. Ginnevra hoisted her weapons and limped back to her cottage.

Her leg burned with pain by the time she reached the cottage, and she was sweating and seeing double every other step. Rather than go inside, she fell heavily onto the bench and dropped the arquebus and mace beside her. She breathed deeply and slowly until her vision returned to normal and her leg didn't feel quite so much like it was being cut off by a rusty saw. Then she pushed herself upright and entered.

Eodan sat by the fire, pressing a folded cloth to his side. Ginnevra stopped. There were scratches across his bare chest, though none very deep, and he had the beginnings of a black eye and bruises all down his left side. "Oh," she said. "I didn't realize. So, the injuries transfer, then?"

"Unfortunately," Eodan said. He reached for a length of bandage to wrap the folded cloth to his body.

Ginnevra hesitated for a moment, then said, "Let me do that." She took the bandage from his hands and passed it around his torso a few times before tying it off. His body was powerfully muscled, as she'd seen when he took off his shirt to change shape, with wiry black hair covering his chest and old scars making pale lines over his ribs and his left shoulder. She averted her eyes, not wanting to be caught staring.

"Thank you," Eodan said when she was finished. He pulled his shirt on, a little stiffly, and said, "How badly did you hurt yourself?"

"Not at all," Ginnevra said. "It's nothing. I heal fast."

Eodan's eyebrows raised, but he said nothing in response to her blatant lie.

"I told the villagers your howl was the maligna," Ginnevra said in an attempt to distract him. "But I'm not sure they believed me. It might be safest if you moved on." The words filled her with a cold ache she ignored.

"You're almost certainly going to have a relapse," Eodan said. "I'm not leaving until you're well."

"How much good can you do me if the villagers hunt and kill you?" Ginnevra shot back.

"I'm not afraid of villagers who can't band together to kill their own monsters." Eodan poured himself a cup of water and drank it down in one gulp. "Are you thirsty?"

Ginnevra scowled, but accepted a cup. She did feel lightheaded and a little sick, though the water helped, but she was sure Eodan was wrong about her relapsing. "Where will you go from here? Not that I'm saying you will leave right away, because you're stubborn and have no common sense."

Eodan settled on a stool. "East, again. There are still members of my pack who could be in danger. After that, I don't know. South for the winter, eventually."

It sounded like a lonely life, but Ginnevra didn't want to say that and sound patronizing or pitying. "I'm not sure how much longer I'll stay here. It's past time I figured out why Arrus is so appealing to monsters, and stop the threat permanently. But that will have to be after I'm fully healed. Another three or four days."

Eodan's lips quirked up at the corners. "Optimistic. I think it will be more like six days."

"And you know this, how?"

Eodan poured himself another cup of water. "I tended the sick among my people before I was outcast."

"You're a physician? No wonder you knew how to care for me." She looked at his hands, so large and yet so agile, and could easily imagine him as such.

"Humans and werewolves—werewolves in their human state— are almost identical. We run hotter than humans, and our bodies are not as fragile, and even in our human forms our sense of smell is exceptional. And, obviously, we have that reaction to silver. Aside from that, the anatomy and disease responses are all the same. So it's not such a stretch." Eodan sipped his water this time.

"Then I'm especially grateful it was you who came to my rescue." It was easier, all the time, not to think of Eodan as a dangerous monster. Ginnevra hoped it didn't mean she was going soft. "I need to sleep now. Thank you for fighting alongside me. We made a good team."

Eodan saluted her with his cup. "It's probably the first time a human and a werewolf have ever fought as one. Too bad no one else can know how we've made history."

Ginnevra chuckled and limped away to her bed.

EIGHT

Ginnevra rose before dawn three days later, on the first day of the month, to celebrate the new moon. Her wound barely hurt at all after three days of quiet and no exertion. She would have to point out to Eodan that she'd been right about her recuperative powers, but later. At the moment, she had more serious business.

She carried the bench a short distance from the cottage and set it to face east, toward the forest. The sky was a faded blue in that direction, the tops of the trees outlined in rosy pink, and the stars had disappeared from that quarter. A brisk wind blew from the north, surprisingly cold; she anticipated a rainstorm later that day. Long after her devotions were over.

She set down the basket containing a bundle of fresh lavender, a stubby black candle in a brass holder, a glass bottle of water, and a couple of oat muffins on the bench and unfolded the cloak she hadn't used since coming to Arrus. It smelled of winter, of wood smoke and roasted meat and snow, and she took a moment to breathe in the scents before settling it around her shoulders.

In the distance, the trees danced in the wind. Keeping the candle lit might be difficult. Ginnevra seated herself on the bench and moved the basket to where she could reach it easily. She put up her hood and pulled it far forward to shield her face, making the roar of the wind diminish enough it didn't echo in her ears. Then she sat for a moment with her eyes closed, breathing slowly as the air filled her lungs, in and out, back and forth. She pictured it as a purple-blue stream she drew in that warmed within her and left her body as a bright red trail.

When her whole body hummed with rhythmic breathing, Ginnevra reached into the basket without looking and pulled out the bundle of lavender. She raised it to her nose and with her other hand crushed some of the flowers. The light scent grew richer, more potent. She breathed it in deeply, holding her breath for a count of seven before expelling it so it blew away the remaining smell. She repeated this three more times, each time holding her breath a little longer, then set the bundle on her lap and looked at the skies. Not much longer now.

She picked up the candle holder and whispered, "*By Your grace I wield the fire.*" A tiny spark kindled on the candle wick. She quickly shielded it with her hand and watched it grow stronger until it warmed her hand. Ginnevra rose and held the candle up, still shielding its flame, in the direction of the moon's rising. The new moon tugged at her, reminding her of the connection she had to the Goddess.

With the candle flame scorching her fingers, she sang quickly:
Where there is fire, She is there
Where there is life, She has care
Where there is illness, She abides
Where there is darkness, She does not hide.
I am her hands, her feet, her eyes
I will not rest 'til battle's end.
Swift to the challenge, until I die
To fight, to conquer, and to defend.
As she sang the second to the last line, the sun peeked over the trees, sending a wave of golden light across their canopy. Ginnevra's

eyes watered from looking almost directly at it. Slowly, she lowered the candle and held it in front of her face, waiting.

There it was—the unmistakable pull of the new moon rising. Ginnevra couldn't see it past the sun's radiance, but seeing didn't matter. She blew out the candle, set it aside, and closed her eyes again, listening to the blood thrumming through her ears like a distant tide.

"Dark Lady," she murmured, "I still don't know what lesson this village has to teach me, but I feel I've done good here, and I am grateful for the opportunity. Thank You."

She breathed in deeply and let out her breath in a great whoosh. "I also don't know what it means that I've come to call a werewolf 'friend.' There is so much I don't understand, like how his people can be called monsters when they mean no one any harm—the ones who turn their backs on Your bright enemy, at any rate—or what will happen when it's time for me to move on. If I may ask a boon for the new month, grant me wisdom to recognize the paths before me, and peaceful welcome to the path I choose."

She listened, but still heard nothing but her own body's rhythms. She'd never heard the Goddess speak, and didn't really expect an answer, but she felt at peace, and that was as much of an answer as she felt worthy of. "And, finally, I don't know if this is appropriate, but I wish You would consider the plight of the werewolves. I can't believe it's justice to leave them outcast. I'll never tell You Your business, of course, but if it's in Your power, it would be nice for You to watch over them."

She brushed her fingers over the smooth surface of the black pearl and bowed her head. "I pledge myself anew to Your service, and swear to keep my oaths. Grant me a strong body, an agile mind, and a valiant heart, ever in Your name." The ritual words filled her with joy and peace.

She pulled back her hood and sat once more. The wind still blew briskly, but the rising sun warmed her face, and she felt comfortable rather than too cold. She picked up the bottle of water and saluted the moon, invisible in the sun's radiance, then drank deeply. Cool and clean, it tasted better than water from an ordinary well—an illusion, since she'd filled the bottle from the bucket drawn from the villagers' well. She wanted to believe it was the ceremony that did it, roused all her senses so everything felt new and alive. Such a wonderful way to welcome in a new month.

She took a bite of an oat muffin and savored its texture and the hint of sweetness. It was a little dry from being yesterday's baking, but nothing unpleasant. She chewed, and let her mind drift. Another day, and she would be fully healed, so there, Eodan! And then she could turn her attention to finding a real solution for the people of Arrus. She'd been on the defensive for far too long. Time to seek out answers.

She sensed Eodan's approach, the faint musk of the werewolf and his nearly silent steps. She wondered if his usual stealthiness was a werewolf thing, or just him. When he was close enough for speech, she said, "Best wishes for a new month."

"Our timekeeping centers on the full moon," Eodan said. "I hope I'm not intruding."

"No, my prayers are done." Ginnevra moved the basket. "Did you eat? I have another muffin."

"Thanks." He took the muffin, but didn't immediately take a bite. "What do you pray for, if it's not rude to ask?"

Ginnevra felt uncomfortable telling him she'd prayed on behalf of his people. "Oh, for understanding, and wisdom. For the chance to use my talents on the Goddess's behalf. For...for the welfare of others I care about."

Eodan bowed his head. "Your faith is nothing like anything I've experienced. If werewolves pray for anything, it's that the Bright Goddess's attention stay far from us. And that whatever destiny she has chosen for us not take us too far from what we hold dear."

He sounded so bleak Ginnevra's heart ached for him. "Do you believe you have a destiny, then?"

"I don't know anymore. I thought, before I was outcast—before my pack committed itself to the Bright Goddess's service—that not worshipping her meant not receiving her dubious blessings, including a destiny." Eodan sighed and bit into his muffin. "But if she had the power to force us to fight against our will in the war, she probably has the power to mold us to her pleasure," he added when his mouth was clear.

"That's frightening, to know someone has that much power over you." Ginnevra finished her muffin and drank more water, then passed the bottle to Eodan. She wanted to say more, but she remembered his anger when she'd pressed him on the subject of injustice to werewolves and held her tongue.

"We're used to it," Eodan said, smiling. He drank, and said, "Where did that water come from? It tastes different."

"I'd say it's the influence of the new moon, but really it's that the glass gives it a different flavor than a wood cup." Ginnevra unfastened her cloak and let it fall in a puddle around her. "I'm nearly healed, by the way."

"Yes, and I'm sure you'll gloat about being right." Eodan finished off the water. "You recover faster even than a werewolf." The black eye he'd gotten fighting the maligna was little more than a shadow now.

"I wasn't going to gloat." She'd meant to, but him bringing it up made it less fun. "What I was really going to say was that it's time I figured out what's bringing all the monsters to Arrus."

Eodan eyed her suspiciously. "That sounds like you're gearing up for a fight."

"I might be. I don't know." Ginnevra looked at the distant forest. "When I first arrived, I thought I'd be fighting off monsters all day long, based on the reports we had. But it was seven days before anything attacked the village, and even then it was only a squasc."

"I don't know what that is."

Ginnevra waved her hand dismissively. "They look like small, furry humans with long ears and fat bodies. They can be vicious, but usually they won't go where humans are. I thought the one I killed had just gotten confused, but now I wonder." She remembered her momentary feeling of pity for the thing and felt uncomfortable, as if she should have found a better solution than cleaving it in two.

Eodan turned the glass bottle restlessly in his hands. "Wonder what?"

"Whether something else isn't going on. When I stumbled on you and Colc in the woods, I thought I had my answer. Werewolves are top predators, and I thought maybe the monster attacks had stopped because they'd all fled from you. But you said you were chasing Colc, which means you'd only just arrived in the area, and that couldn't be the reason."

"I noticed the woods around here were very empty of any living creatures," Eodan said.

"You did? Do you know how far?"

Eodan shrugged. "I don't know human measurements of distance, sorry. But at least as far as I can run in half a day."

"I wish I knew what that meant." She sighed. "I talked to the villagers when I first arrived, trying to get a sense for if there was a pattern to the attacks or something, and they all agreed there had never been more than the rarest monster appearances up until two weeks before they complained to the Principessa of Talagne, which means a month before I arrived. So something happened to start the problem, and something else happened to...I don't want to say 'stop it,' because I don't think it's gone away, not if something like a maligna is still in the area to attack."

"Suppress it, maybe," Eodan suggested.

"That's a good word. Anyway, I have no idea what might have started the problem, but I think my arrival may have been what suppressed it. Monsters aren't stupid—"

"Thank you," Eodan said dryly.

"I don't consider you a monster anymore, but you're not stupid either, and you're fishing for compliments." Ginnevra pretended to glare at him. "The point is, monsters have good instincts for how much of a threat another monster is, or a human. If they found out I was here, they'd avoid this place."

"But the maligna didn't."

"Malignae are strong enough to think they have a chance against a paladin. Or a werewolf. And that one acted desperate. I think it was starving and needed food more than it cared about safety." Ginnevra looked at the forest again. "But that's beside the point. I need to find out what has the monsters in this area so worked up. Because I could be wrong, and the reason the monsters stopped attacking is that there are no more monsters. That something made them all flee westward, and it was just coincidence that I arrived as the last of them left."

"You don't believe that," Eodan said.

She shook her head. "If something happened in the forest, if it was a one-time event, like a lightning strike, more monsters would find their way in. But the forest is far too quiet. I've only been in there a few times, but it always feels empty. I think that means that whatever it was is still going on, or still exerts an influence. And anything strong enough to scare monsters is a potential threat to humans."

"And a threat to you." Eodan looked calm, but there was an edge to his voice Ginnevra was surprised by.

"I suppose," she said, "but that's what I do. I kill monsters. It doesn't matter if it's a threat to me."

Eodan's lips tightened briefly. "I mean that you don't have even the smallest sense of self-preservation. You're planning to head into the woods with nothing but your sword, no idea what creature you face or what it might do—"

"Of course I have a sense of self-preservation! I can't be a useful paladin if I'm careless and get killed at the first encounter with danger. Yes, I intend to hunt this thing, whatever it is—it might not even be a creature, you know—but I'll assess it and understand its weaknesses before I throw myself at it headlong." His casual assumption that she was careless made her angry, but worse than that, it sent a pang of sorrow through her that he didn't respect her skills or her good sense.

"Then I'm coming with you."

Ginnevra bit back her first hasty response, which was *The hell you are*. Eodan did not look like someone interested in arguing. He looked like a force of nature, a storm pent up in a human body, with his brow furrowed and his lips once more set in a tight, straight line and his arms folded across his chest so the muscles bulged. Instead, she said, "It's not your responsibility."

"Why should it have to be my responsibility? You'll be more effective if you're not fighting alone."

"Paladins work together because we're trained for it. We study and practice how to fight as a unit. You and I, we don't know each other's fighting abilities. We'd just fumble over each other and maybe get one or both of us killed." Even as she spoke, she'd started going over possibilities in her head. Eodan was a powerful fighter, she'd seen him kill the maligna, and it would be comforting not to go into danger alone. But she couldn't let him risk himself like that when he wasn't a trained paladin.

"If you leave me behind, I'll just follow you. There's no creature in the world that can hide from a hunting werewolf, however stealthy you are." Eodan glared at her more intently. "You know you don't want to do this alone."

It was true, she didn't. She tried one last time. "You're not trained for this. If you get yourself killed, it will be my fault."

"I'm not a weakling, Ginnevra. I'm an experienced hunter, I know how to move silently, and I've killed monsters before." Eodan's blue eyes were fierce on her. "Stop arguing. When are we going?"

Ginnevra closed her eyes and silently cursed. "Tomorrow, or day after. I want to be sure I'm healed before I head off into peril with a companion who may get himself killed on my watch."

Eodan grinned. "You paladins are so optimistic."

Ginnevra shook her head, but she couldn't stop smiling in return. She rose and said, "I'm going into the village to talk to people. I never thought to ask for specific details about what things were like before the monster incursion, how the monsters attacked and what kind they were. And it disturbs me that some of the villagers killed by monsters were killed in the forest, not near the village. The woman who owned the cottage before I showed up, for one."

"Why does that matter?" Eodan stood, bringing the basket with him.

"If they knew the forest was dangerous, they wouldn't have entered it. I want to know whether those deaths happened before the monster attacks became serious or after."

"You believe whatever stirred up the monsters might have killed those people."

"You really are smart for a monster. Yes, I want to know the timing." Ginnevra sighed. "I should have asked these questions sooner, but I made assumptions and let those rule my actions." She picked up the bench and carried it as they walked back to the cottage.

"It's not too late," Eodan said. "Probably."

Ginnevra rolled her eyes. "It seems werewolves are optimistic, too. Thanks for not relieving my mind."

"It's a gift," Eodan said.

CHAPTER
NINE

A day later, feeling herself whole enough to face a serious challenge, Ginnevra limbered up before dressing for battle. She eyed her plate armor as she stretched. Once again, she was going into danger without its protection. But in a scouting situation, she needed silence more than she needed solid steel, and despite the Goddess's gift of stealthiness, the plate always creaked more than Ginnevra was comfortable with. Eodan had also said it reeked of silver, and if there was a chance this threat was capable of sensing that sort of thing, she didn't want to give them away.

So instead she put on her chainmail as well as her steel vambraces, as a compromise, and wore her padded coif to give her a little extra protection and keep her hair out of her eyes. She pulled on her gloves and snugged them close against her fingers, then flexed her hands to test the fit. It was a nervous little ritual of hers for when she was going into unknown danger, a reminder that she had the skills and the knowledge to face any foe.

She ran her gloved fingers over her grace and said a quick, unspoken prayer, not for success—that would be like asking for a given future—but for strength and quickness and understanding. Those were enough to let her make the future she wanted.

Eodan waited in the front room. He was dressed as he always was, in the ill-fitting shirt and trousers, and Ginnevra impulsively asked, "Where did you get those clothes?"

"I stole them from the village," Eodan said without a trace of guilt. "It was either that or be naked while I took care of you."

Ginnevra blushed. "It wasn't a criticism, I just—never mind."

"I understand." Eodan opened the door. "That was a busy night, the night you were wounded. I bandaged your leg and then worked that chainmail off you so I could carry you here. Then I made you a bed on the floor and left you to go find these clothes. And *then* I had to go back to the forest with a sack to collect your chainmail, as I assumed you wouldn't want it left lying around. Fortunately, I could handle your sword without trouble."

Ginnevra nodded. "You went out of your way to help a stranger not even of your own kind. Thank you. In case I didn't say it before."

"You did, but I didn't do it to be thanked. What is it you say—it was my honor to serve? Or is that blasphemous for someone not a paladin to say?"

"It's not. Though most people don't think that way." Ginnevra shrugged her sword over her shoulder and followed him outside. It was about an hour after noon, and the dark moon sailed high above. Ginnevra had chosen this time not just because the sunlight might keep the monsters at bay, but because the moon was like a blessing on their venture.

They crossed the untilled fields to the tree line. Tall grasses, yellow even at this time of year, swished around Ginnevra's ankles. Farther south, the road left Arrus and led toward the woods, narrowing to something more like a path. Ginnevra saw a villager in the distance and waved. She had no idea what that person was doing so far from the village, but she hoped he or she was sensible enough to stay away from the forest despite the inviting path. Aside from the villager, she saw no movement, not even squirrels or birds. "It's unsettling," she said.

"Too quiet," Eodan agreed. "It's as if even the trees know something is wrong, with how still their branches are."

Ginnevra nodded. The warm, dry air was scented with the green smell of leaves and the richer scent of the undergrowth. Ginnevra didn't know anything about plants, but these smelled like mint mixed with lemon, a nice odor that mingled with Eodan's musky scent in a pleasant way. She recalled how awful Colc had smelled and said, "Does each werewolf have a distinct smell? Because Colc didn't smell like you."

"I've noticed the werewolves sworn to the Bright Goddess have a sweeter odor," Eodan said. "Like decomposition. It's disgusting."

"Very." She wondered if he felt uncomfortable at her referring so casually to his smell, whether he knew that for humans having a strong body odor was usually a bad thing. She was used to the werewolf musk after all this time, and if she was honest with herself, she could admit she found it pleasant. That made *her* feel uncomfortable. It was one thing being Eodan's friend, but she wasn't sure it was right for a paladin to become complacent about non-humans. It wasn't something she liked thinking about.

They entered the forest directly east of the cottage, where the trees didn't grow quite so closely together. After a dozen steps, Ginnevra muttered the invocation to conjure her sense of true north, and Eodan said, "Did you say something?"

"Just working a small magic." The little tugging sensation in her chest grew stronger, and then her awareness of it faded into a subconscious pull. "It's so I don't get lost in the forest."

"Werewolves have an innate sense of direction," Eodan said. "I didn't realize it was something paladins could have."

"Anyone with a grace," Ginnevra corrected him. "Any of the villagers can do it. Or light fires, or mend small things. There are a handful of small magics the Goddess blesses us with."

"I continue to be amazed at your relationship with your creator."

Eodan stopped. They were well within the trees now, the light dim as it filtered through the branches. "I'm going to change now."

"Oh." Ginnevra turned her back on him.

Eodan laughed. "Werewolves don't have a nudity taboo. That would be impossible. You don't have to be embarrassed." She heard the rustle of fabric, loud against the silence.

"I'm not embarrassed," she lied, "and werewolves might not have that taboo, but humans do, and I'm human. So I'm giving you as much privacy as I can manage."

"All right." He still sounded amused, and Ginnevra tried to get her blush under control.

After another moment, Eodan padded around to face her. Whatever his change entailed, it was perfectly silent. She wished briefly she could see it, though not if it meant seeing him naked, of course. Eodan sat and looked up at her. She had the suspicion he was still laughing.

"Stay close," she told him, though he knew that because they'd discussed the strategy that morning. They would go deep into the forest, searching for any sign of monsters—or of a thing monsters might be afraid of.

Eodan nodded. Ginnevra shrugged her shoulders to settle her sword more firmly, and they set off eastward.

To her enhanced hearing, they sounded like a couple of ungainly children, crashing through the scant undergrowth and crushing old leaf fall and twigs underfoot. It was her imagination; she had the stealth of a moonless night in her soul, and Eodan was as quiet as any creature his size could be. Quieter, maybe, as he had the intelligence to walk wide of anything that might be especially noisy. But walking through the woods, intent on finding a mysterious enemy, Ginnevra wished they could be as silent as the breezes that occasionally brushed her cheeks.

She thought once more on the villager she'd seen just now. She'd gotten the impression that the villagers didn't enter the forest anymore, not since two of them had been killed within its boundaries. But that person—she thought it had been a man—had been headed that direction. He was either brave or stupid. Possibly both. She decided not to worry about him. She couldn't stand over every villager and ensure his safety, even if that were the kind of thing paladins did, and if he wanted to take a chance on danger, that was his choice.

Instead, she reviewed what she'd learned from the villagers the day before, cringing inside at how stupid she'd been not to ask those questions sooner. It might have changed how she approached this task of protecting Arrus. Maghinardo hadn't acted surprised when she'd asked about the villagers killed in the forest, nor when she'd wanted to know what kind of monster attacks they'd seen before her arrival. He seemed to think of her as some kind of divine force rather than as a woman with special skills. Ginnevra was more than ever grateful for the little cottage that gave her some privacy, because she was sure the villagers would have fawned over her if she'd had to stay in the tavern.

Now she reviewed the facts in her head. The monster attacks had started small, with pixies pestering the children and stealing food left unsupervised. Annoying, but not dangerous. But they'd gotten gradually worse from there. It turned out the villagers used to go into the forest sometimes for wood and wild plants, and they all reported sightings of dryads slipping from tree to tree, stalking humans and enticing them to follow. Three villagers had gone missing and were never found; two others had been killed by creatures unknown, but by the descriptions of the wounds Ginnevra suspected the dog-like beasts called krokottas, spotted like cats but with ridged backs and muzzles like hunting dogs. They were scavengers most of the time, but good enough hunters if their usual prey was unavailable.

She felt confident of this guess because a pack of krokottas then took up residence in the area, at first just hanging around the village outskirts, but then growing bolder and attacking villagers, in one case dragging a child away. The child's parents had rescued her, but she'd lost most of one arm. Another child hadn't been rescued in time.

Then came the monsters Ginnevra didn't recognize from the villagers' descriptions, mainly because they had attacked at night and the villagers hadn't seen them clearly. One might have been a basilisk, but with nobody turned to stone, she couldn't be sure. Maghinardo had told her of creatures clawing at doors or windows, shrieks and moans like lost spirits, a hissing sound Ginnevra deeply hoped was not a lamia. Food and drink left outside was either taken or fouled. All the animals had to be kept indoors at night. She could well understand why the villagers had sent for help.

And then, the night before Ginnevra arrived, the attacks stopped. Ginnevra had gone on watch every day, the people had continued vigilant against monstrous foes, but nothing had happened until the squasc got itself trapped in the well.

She still wasn't sure she believed her presence had caused the difference, and she wasn't sure how she could prove it one way or the other. For now, she was going to go with the other possibility: that something had happened in the forest to drive the monsters into civilized country, and something else had happened to make them disappear.

Despite the unnatural silence, the walk was pleasant, the forest cool and comfortable. It reminded her of years long past, of playing at monster hunting with her brothers in the overgrown field near her parents' home. Ginnevra glanced down at Eodan and wondered what he was thinking. It was too bad he couldn't speak in that form. Of course, they shouldn't carry on a conversation if they wanted to sneak up on their unknown enemy, so that was a pointless wish.

She continued scanning her surroundings, looking for signs that animals or monsters had passed this way. There weren't many dead leaves underfoot this early in the year, but what there was showed little signs of disturbance. Most of what she saw was weeks old, and she wasn't a good enough tracker to identify the creatures who'd passed through beyond wolf and deer and monster. "Do you see tracks? Fresh ones?" she murmured.

Eodan shook his head. He didn't appear to be tracking anything, but Ginnevra could guess at the sensitivity of his nose and assumed he learned more than she did from the faint tracks.

They walked for some time, more than an hour, Ginnevra thought, heading roughly east and a little south. Despite her internal resolve, Ginnevra was bored. She mentally slapped herself out of complacency and walked a little faster. Maybe they needed a different search pattern. Maybe they should head farther south, or circle around to where the road entered the forest. She hadn't seen the villagers use it, but it might be something the monsters had lit on as a marker guiding them toward human prey.

She opened her mouth to express these thoughts and caught a whiff of something unfamiliar. It smelled unpleasantly sweet, like overripe fruit, something between a peach and an apple. With it came, more faintly, a hint of wood smoke.

She stopped and turned with her nose in the air like a hunting hound, seeking out the source. East, and south—just where they'd been going. "I don't recognize that smell, but the wood smoke might be a traveler, or group of travelers," she said. She didn't bother asking if Eodan had smelled it. "I'd like to know if they've seen anything. And they might need warning, though I'm beginning to think there aren't any monsters left in this forest."

Eodan nodded and trotted away. She hurried to keep up with him.

The smells grew stronger as they ran, with the smoke soon over-powering the sweet odor. Ginnevra rearranged her assumptions. They might be running toward a forest fire, though she heard no sound of flames, so she found that unlikely. But whatever it was must be big, and she couldn't guess what human or group of humans would come all the way out here to light a bonfire.

Eodan stopped abruptly, and Ginnevra nearly tripped over him. "Wh—"

Then she heard it, a rustling, slithering noise just out of sight ahead that sent a chill through Ginnevra. It sounded like scales rubbing against stone. Ginnevra touched her grace and prayed fervently it wasn't a lamia. The half-serpent women were strong and fast and had the ability to fascinate their prey while they looped the coils of their lower bodies around them to strangle them to death. Ginnevra was proof against their fascination, but she didn't think Eodan was. And if this was a lamia, by the sound it was the biggest one Ginnevra had ever encountered.

She gestured to Eodan to circle around south while she headed north. They needed more information, even if that meant being separated for a short while. Eodan ran off without hesitation. Ginnevra thought about drawing her sword, decided she would rather have both hands free for now, and continued north.

The smoky scent was strong enough Ginnevra didn't know why she hadn't seen any actual smoke. The rustling, slithering sound didn't change in volume or intensity, but she had a very clear idea of where the creature making it was. She continued circling, threading her way between the oak trees, watching for a surprise attack and for Eodan.

Then the noise stopped. A loud sigh filled the air, and the smoky smell was briefly overridden by the sweet odor. Ginnevra's curiosity was at the breaking point. Carefully, she crept closer. The trees here grew close together, never thinned by logging or fire, and she couldn't see past the closest rank of tree trunks. That meant her enemy likely couldn't see her, but Ginnevra never liked to count on possibilities.

The trees thinned out before she reached the clearing, and she stopped well before she would enter it. Something moved beyond the oaks. Something big. It was the same color as the tree trunks, a grayish-brown streaked with black. Ginnevra's relief that it wasn't a lamia, which were always brightly colored, faded when she realized she had no idea what it might be.

Slipping from tree trunk to tree trunk, Ginnevra edged closer.

The creature stopped moving, and Ginnevra froze, fearing she'd been seen. But nothing came surging through the forest bent on killing her. When the creature next moved, it was with a ponderousness, almost like it had rolled over in sleep. She hadn't considered that the creature might be asleep, though it made sense if it was nocturnal as so many monsters were. That changed nothing. She still had to be cautious.

The edge of the clearing was visible now, past a final rank of trees. Ginnevra chose the fattest of them and slipped into its shadow. Then she peered out around it to get her first look at the creature.

She'd been wrong about no fires devastating this forest. The clearing was a natural glen made wider by a long-ago fire that had cut a gash across it running southward. It was easily two hundred feet across at its widest point and covered with bracken and black-berry bushes, their fruit not yet ripe. Smoke filled the air, rising from piles of brambles covered by hunks of damp thatch that made a ragged line dividing the clearing in half east-west. The smoke rising from the piles was gray and thick, drifting eastward on the light breeze.

The drifting smoke drew Ginnevra's gaze east. At first, she thought loggers had been at work, because a mass of dark grayish-brown wood lay in a pile off to the eastern side of the clearing. Then she realized the mass was moving lightly, like a giant creature breathing. The color was right, but it couldn't be logs, because the shape was too irregular. Whatever it was, it was taller than she by a foot or more, and longer than it was tall.

More details came into focus: a fat, serpentine tail curled loosely around its hindquarters; powerful back legs pulled in against its scaly body; a wedge-shaped head, crowned with pale horns, resting on skinny forelimbs. Then it shifted again, and Ginnevra covered her mouth to hold in a gasp as a wing the size of a bedspread lifted slightly and drifted down again. She'd never seen anything like it before. No one had in over a century.

But it was definitely a dragon.

CHAPTER

TEN

Ginnevra instinctively ducked behind the tree and clung to it, controlling her frightened breathing. Dragons were dangerous, with their knife-edged claws and teeth like daggers and almost impenetrable hide. There were stories of paladins fighting dragons, but all of them involved entire companies attacking and killing the monsters. One paladin alone didn't stand a chance.

To distract herself, she examined the smoking brambles. Those had been set on purpose, and by the way they were distributed, they were intended to do something to the dragon. Ginnevra had a sudden image of Beccio, one of the villagers, and his beehives. He used smoke to dull the bees' senses so they wouldn't attack or panic when he moved their hives or harvested the honeycombs. Maybe dragons were susceptible to the same tactic.

She peered around the other side of the tree at the dragon. Its oddly-streaked hide made it difficult for her to make out features, but it did seem to be asleep. Greenish gas trickled from its nostrils, not much more than a fine thread, but enough that Ginnevra could tell it was the source of the sickly sweet odor.

Movement at the far side of the clearing caught her eye, a black shape low to the ground. She waved to get Eodan's attention and pointed westward. Eodan nodded and disappeared into the trees.

Ginnevra worked her way carefully around the clearing, staying within the tree line, but keeping an eye on the dragon in case it was a ruse and the thing was just waiting for its moment to attack. It never moved except once, and that was to roll onto its side, its front legs pulled up beneath its chin, which made it look like a sleeping cat—a deadly dangerous sleeping cat. With wings.

She heard Eodan approaching and realized he was human again in time to keep her gaze locked well above ground level. A part of her said she was being ridiculous, that nudity didn't matter when they were dealing with a dragon, but the rest of her clung to her modesty taboos.

Eodan, for his part, looked completely unconcerned about his nakedness. He beckoned her to move deeper into the woods and then stood close enough that not looking lower than his waist was easy. "Someone's keeping it contained," he murmured, quietly enough even her enhanced hearing barely made out his words.

"Yes, but it doesn't make sense," Ginnevra whispered back. "If it's the villagers, why would they trap a dragon and then send for a paladin who might discover their secret? And if it's not the villagers, who else lives out here that could manage something this big? Those smokers—if you can call them that, at their size—they're the work of several people."

"I'm more interested in learning how they knew it would work." Eodan looked toward the clearing. "Do humans know that much about dragons? Because werewolves don't."

"I would have sworn not. Dragons aren't mythical, but it's been over a hundred years since anyone's seen one. And last time, it was a company of paladins that killed it, not a handful of villagers smoking it into unconsciousness." Ginnevra scowled in thought. "Whoever this is, either they couldn't kill it and are keeping it subdued instead, or they're keeping it subdued because they want something from it."

"I hadn't thought of the second possibility," Eodan said. "What do dragons have that humans want?"

Ginnevra shrugged. "Treasure, maybe. I don't know if the legends about dragon hoards are true. Not wisdom, because they aren't much more intelligent than a dog. If you could skin it, you could make dragon hide armor that would be tougher and lighter than plate. And I've heard some people believe dragon body parts have restorative powers, but I'm not sure what those powers are."

"But they're keeping it alive, so that must not be it. My bet is on treasure. Even if the rumors aren't true, that's an incredible incentive."

Ginnevra turned and walked toward the clearing. "I need a closer look."

Quicker than thought, Eodan stepped in front of her, blocking her way. "That's madness. If it wakes up, it could kill you."

"I don't think it's going to wake up. Go ahead, change. We need more information."

Eodan didn't budge. "We need to stay away from it. I may not know much about dragons, but I know they're erratic and vicious and quick to attack. Let's go to the village and roust people until they tell us what's going on."

"Questioning the villagers will be more effective if I've already learned things." Her fear had vanished in the prospect of taking action. "Those smokers might keep it unconscious, but that doesn't explain how someone trapped it here in the first place. It had to come from somewhere, after all. Either stop complaining and change, or wait here."

Eodan scowled and threw up his hands. "Are all paladins mad, or is it just you?"

"We prefer to think of it as 'selectively sane.' And it brings us success." Ginnevra stepped around him and made her way quietly back to the tree line. Shortly, Eodan joined her, once more in wolf shape.

Nothing had changed. The dragon still lay sprawled cat-like on its side. The threads of greenish gas were a little thicker than before, and now Ginnevra could smell the sickly sweet odor over the wood smoke. She noted the positions of the bramble piles, how they effectively made a wall between the dragon and the rest of the clearing. She shrugged the scabbard off her shoulder and drew her blade, brushed her fingers across her grace in a silent prayer for strength, and stepped out from between the trees.

Moving silently through the bracken was a challenge even for her skills, as the thriving ferns brushed her ankles and swept past her shins, making a rustling noise. Beside her, Eodan seemed to have no trouble keeping quiet. But the dragon didn't react as if it heard them. Its breathing sounded like someone pouring gravel between two buckets, raspy and loud. Its hind legs twitched once, again like a cat's, and then it returned to lying still.

Ginnevra paused at the line of smoking brambles, examining them. As she'd observed, damp piles of thatch lay over the brambles, which appeared to be uprooted blackberry bushes. Fires smoldered in the heart of each patch, struggling for air. She fingered a handful of thatch, trying to guess how recently it had been dampened. It felt sticky, as if something besides water had been poured on it. She sniffed her fingers, but smelled nothing unusual. She eased past the bramble, keeping out of the smoke cloud, and walked forward.

The air beyond grew cloudier as she neared the dragon, dizzying her and making her feel a little sleepy. She breathed shallowly, trying not to inhale too much smoke. It burned her eyes and made her long to cough. She hoped Eodan, lower to the ground, was having less trouble than she was.

The dragon was smaller than her first glance had told her, but that still made it enormous—taller than she was at its shoulder and twice as long. Its belly scales were a dirty cream color, lighter than the rest of its body, that matched the four curved horns on its head. Ginnevra worked her way around to its tail, hoping for a better glimpse of its wings, which lay folded along its back. Nothing about this made sense. It wasn't a hatchling, so it hadn't been born here, but if it had come from somewhere else, why hadn't it flown away again before someone had set up the smokers?

The dragon's sides heaved with its breathing, not very rapidly, but deeply, as if it relished the smell of the smoke. Ginnevra was seized with a desire to touch it, to see if the scales felt smooth or rough. She controlled the urge and took another step.

Eodan growled a warning that made her jerk her attention away from the dragon. He had his legs splayed wide as if he needed the stance to keep his balance, but his muzzle pointed at the edge of the clearing, at the gash cutting across the southern end. "What did you see?" she asked without thinking.

Eodan shook his head and trotted in that direction, not very fast and weaving slightly. Ginnevra searched the tree line for any sign of danger. Still no animals or birds, and no monsters.

She turned back to examine the dragon's wings and was in time to see it lift its head and open enormous glowing yellow eyes.

She sucked in an incautious breath and choked on the smoke, coughing loudly. Instantly the dragon rose up on its forelimbs and snaked its long neck around toward her. Green gas trickled from its mouth and nostrils, the scent of which was almost overpowering. Feeling even more like falling asleep, Ginnevra retreated as quickly as she dared without turning her back on the dragon. Behind her, Eodan let out a howl of warning, but she didn't dare look to see what he was worried about.

The dragon's head tilted, almost curiously, and its mouth opened. Ginnevra guessed its next move in time to draw in another deep, sweet-smoky scented lungful of air and hold it just before it exhaled a cloud of poisonous gas almost in her face.

She dropped, rolled awkwardly over her sword, and came to her hands and knees just at the line of burning brambles. The dragon let out a strange sound, a coughing, hacking wheeze too quiet to be called a roar. Green gas filled the air above Ginnevra, and she scrambled one-handed to get out of the cloud, not caring anymore about the dragon's approach. Her eyes watered painfully, her skin felt tight and dry, her lungs were on fire, but she made it to the tree line before needing to breathe again.

She spun and put her back to a tree, gasping for air. It tasted foul, like ditchwater mixed with honey, but it didn't affect her senses or her strength, and most of the gas cloud still hovered where the dragon had breathed it out. Eodan was nowhere in sight. Fear for him overrode fear for herself, and she pushed to her feet, scanning the clearing.

The dragon paced the line of smokers, its head bobbing like a serpent's. Now that it was upright and moving, Ginnevra could see what had been concealed before: one of the dragon's wings drooped awkwardly, dragging along the ground, unlike the other, which the dragon held arched high above its body. Broken. That explained why it hadn't flown away. There were so many other mysteries Ginnevra wasn't all that excited about having figured out one of them.

Movement to the right drew her attention, and she sagged with relief to see Eodan on his feet and looking unharmed, though his fur was matted on one side like he'd rolled in the bracken. "I think we're safe here," she told him when he reached her. "It doesn't want to pass the fires. See, it's falling asleep again." Sure enough, the dragon, after emitting another puff or two of green gas, had staggered away and then sunk to the ground as if its legs wouldn't support it.

Ginnevra gestured, and she and Eodan circled the clearing to the south, away from where they'd entered. The air still stank of the dragon's breath, though Ginnevra judged it simply clung to her skin and clothing and hadn't followed them. It was still an awful stench.

"I want to see how close the road is to this place," she said. She sheathed her sword and slung the strap over her shoulder. "If the villagers venture this far into the woods, they could be in danger."

Eodan stopped and sat back on his haunches. "What?" Ginnevra asked, forgetting again that he couldn't speak.

Eodan's body quivered, and for a moment he was haloed in silver. Then he was human again, crouched in the undergrowth. He didn't stand. "How sure are you that wasn't the point?" he asked.

"You mean, that the villagers did this? It's hard to see an alternative explanation. But it doesn't make sense. Like I said, why would they trap a dragon alive and then send for someone who'd be duty bound to kill it?"

"Why would they want a dragon alive at all?" Eodan shook his head. "That comes back to us not knowing what use a dragon is. Did you see its wing?"

"Yes. It clearly can't fly away." Ginnevra looked back the way they'd come, for a moment imagining the dragon coming after them. "Let's see how far the road is from here, and whether people have been using it recently."

Eodan lowered his head, and the same shimmer wrapped him, disappearing to reveal his wolf shape. He prowled ahead of Ginnevra, his nose low to the ground. Ginnevra let him lead the way, reasoning that his tracking abilities were superior to her own.

They found the road some two hundred feet south of the clearing. It looked even less like a road than it did from the fields outside Arrus; bushes and trees grew close on either side, giving it the appearance of a well-traveled game trail. Eodan paced along it, sniffing and occasionally darting off to the side. The ground was still damp from the previous day's storm, but Ginnevra saw no footprints in the soft earth.

When they neared the edge of the forest, Eodan veered off and ran northward. Ginnevra trotted after him, wondering if he'd caught someone's scent. But he only led her back to where they'd entered the forest and then changed shape, picking up the clothes he'd left in a neatly folded pile. Ginnevra politely turned her back while he dressed.

"The rain yesterday cleared out most of the scents," Eodan said. "I saw traces of human footprints, but not enough to tell how many or who they were. No one's been out there since yesterday."

"Stupid rain," Ginnevra groused. "Let's go back. I don't mind telling you this has me utterly confused."

They walked back across the fields, waving to one of the farmers working his land. This time, no villagers approached the forest. Ginnevra wished now she'd accosted whoever it was she'd seen going there earlier. She had too many questions and not even the beginnings of answers.

Back in the cottage, she sat on a stool and rubbed a hand over her face. "Ugh. I still smell like that gas."

"Yes, and I thought you were dead when it breathed on you," Eodan said irritably. "That had to have been poisonous."

"Probably, but I avoided it, and it's very hard to poison a paladin. I was scared it had gotten you when I didn't see you right away." Ginnevra accepted the cup of water he handed her and gulped it down. She'd never wanted a bath so much in her life.

"I was sensible and stayed away. Besides, I thought I saw something in the forest." Eodan drank from his own cup. "But I got distracted when the dragon moved, and whatever it was got away. I didn't get a good scent from it, but it was big enough it could have been a deer or a human. Whatever it was, it stayed off the road."

Ginnevra nodded. "So. There's a dragon in the forest. That certainly would account for how all the monsters fled, though not for why they fled in such an orderly way, the weakest ones first. But everything that attacked Arrus would have justifiably been terrified of a dragon."

"And that explains why the attacks stopped," Eodan said. "No new monsters would have entered the forest while the dragon was there, so once the existing monsters were cleared out—it sounds like your guess was correct."

"But I don't understand anything else." Ginnevra stood and paced, gesturing to emphasize her words. "It would actually make sense for the villagers to keep the dragon contained so it couldn't do harm, given that none of them are equipped to kill a dragon. But in that case, they should have sent word to Abraciabene so the Blessed would send a whole company to dispose of it. Instead, they keep it a secret and ask for a different kind of help, which also makes no sense because they couldn't know I wouldn't discover the dragon and ruin their plan, whatever it is."

"It makes sense if not all the villagers are in on the secret," Eodan said. "If only some of them know about the dragon, the rest could have innocently interfered without meaning to. Did you get the sense that they were hiding anything?"

Ginnevra scowled. "No, but I think we've established that I didn't approach this situation the way I should have. But even so, nobody in Arrus has ever behaved as if they had a secret they were afraid I'd ferret out. I think it's safe to assume that most of them aren't lying to me."

"Then we're sure it's a few villagers who have a reason to keep a dragon subdued." Eodan poured himself another cup of water. "Which leads us back to—why?"

"Everything we know about dragons is legendary," Ginnevra said. "But we don't have to know if the rumors are fact, we just have to know whether some villagers might believe they're true. And the number one rumor everyone knows about dragons is that they collect treasure. Gold, and silver, and gems. What if our conspirators are keeping the dragon sedated until its wing heals and they can follow it to its lair?"

"That's a big 'if'," Eodan said. "I don't know anything about dragon physiognomy, but bones in general don't heal well unless they're set and immobilized. And I didn't like the way it was dragging its wing. That might be their plan, but I think it's doomed to failure."

"Remember it only matters what they *think* they're doing, right?" Ginnevra licked her lips and grimaced at how they tasted of overripe fruit and drainage water. "Could I get more water, please?"

Eodan refilled her cup and passed it back. "There is one thing," he said. "I didn't notice any carcasses near the dragon. Either it eats its prey whole, or our conspirators haven't been feeding it."

"It must be the former. Why go to all this trouble and then not feed their prize?" Ginnevra opened the front door, rinsed her mouth, and spat. That made her feel better. The next drink of water didn't taste foul. "But now I'm not sure what to do next. I hate to go to Maghinardo and make accusations when I don't know who's behind the scheme. These village headmen are never equipped to exact justice. And I'm not sure what's happening is a crime. If it wasn't for how secretive the whole thing is, I'd let them have their way."

"You think it's right, what they're doing to the dragon?" Eodan sounded appalled, which startled Ginnevra.

"They're not hurting it," she said, "and I could even make a case for them helping it, if their smoke trap keeps it still so it doesn't wrench its broken wing. There's definitely something in the burning thatch that causes sleepiness. And it *is* a monster. It might have destroyed Arrus if it wasn't injured."

"It's trapped, and they want something from it it doesn't want to give. I would have thought that mattered to you," Eodan said.

Ginnevra, about to say something else, was caught off-guard. She never thought of monsters as creatures deserving of the Dark Lady's blessing of free will. Dragons were vicious killers; that was something legend and history agreed on. And yet she had a sudden memory of the dragon lying with its forelegs pulled up like a cat, and she wasn't sure anymore where her duty lay.

"So," she said, keeping her voice level, "you think we ought to figure out how to free it."

Eodan wouldn't meet her eyes. "I don't know. You have a point that it's capable of destroying the village. It just feels wrong."

Ginnevra almost said *Is that because you sympathize with a fellow monster?* but caught herself before she could be mortally insulting. Instead, she said, "I have to consider my duty, Eodan. I'm sworn to protect humans from monsters just like that one."

Eodan stood. "And monsters like me."

He sounded bitterly angry, and it sent a pang through her heart. "Eodan, you're not a monster. Why are you...you seem to care about this dragon's welfare, and I'm not sure why. Surely dragons are as dangerous to your kind as they are to mine?"

"They probably are." Eodan's shoulders sagged. "It's just that they've trapped it, and when it woke up, it didn't look angry, it looked curious. Like it wanted to know what you were. And I was watching when it breathed out gas—you know, in case I needed to drag you to safety—and it was just a normal exhalation. With a ribcage that size, it must have lungs big enough to fill that whole clearing with poison if it wanted. But it didn't."

Ginnevra considered this. "I agree, it didn't move like an attacker. But that might be the effect of the smoke, confusing it. It's not proof."

"It's enough to justify looking closer." Eodan looked as stubborn as he had when he'd insisted on going after the maligna with her. She was beginning to appreciate his adamant will.

"All right," she said. "Even though the sensible thing is to kill it in its sleep."

Eodan turned on her, growling, and she grinned at him and added, "Didn't we establish that I'm not sensible?"

He subsided, looking a little abashed. "Even if it's not a crime, trapping a dragon," he said, "they certainly think it's something they need to hide. We ought to find out why that is."

"I admit I'd rather learn the truth before I expose their secret to the world." Ginnevra pulled off her coif and ran her fingers through her hair, tidying it. "It still doesn't make a lot of sense, but then that's human motivation for you."

"I'd like to say werewolves are more logical, but we howl at the moon three days in every month, so I'm not sure that's a winning argument," Eodan said.

T he smell of the poison gas clung to Ginnevra's clothes and skin. She'd never been so grateful for the protection of the coif that kept her hair free of the stink. Grimacing, she changed into a fresh shirt, hose, and breeches and gathered up her smelly clothing. There was a woman in the village who'd washed Ginnevra's clothes before; that was as good a place as any for her to start asking questions.

Eodan had declined to go with her, saying, "You're the paladin, and I think it would look strange for your brother to be the one asking questions. Besides, I need a bath." Ginnevra hadn't thought he looked or smelled grimy, but she recalled his wolf's matted fur and realized what he meant.

She walked wide of the farmers' fields, not wanting to disturb them as well as being unwilling to engage in conversation. Now that she knew some of the villagers were hiding an enormous secret, she wanted more than ever to control the conversations she had with them. She cursed herself once more for being so careless about this mission, then pushed those thoughts aside. Dwelling on the past was pointless. If she wanted to solve this mystery, she needed to focus on the present.

The afternoon sun beat down on her unprotected head, relaxing her despite herself. She loved the heat of summer, the way it made everything smell warm and welcoming, and today felt like a taste of that rather than late spring. The tall grasses, already dry and yellowing, bent and broke beneath her feet as she trod the fallow space between fields and forest. Now that she didn't need to be stealthy, she liked the noise she made, the rustling, whispering sound like a roomful of worshippers. Celebrating the new moon hadn't been the same without her friends. Well, next month she would likely be with them again.

The thought of returning to her company filled her with a disquiet she couldn't understand. She missed her sister paladins, of course, and missed their camaraderie, but it was nice, being on her own, and she found herself reluctant to give that up. No doubt she'd feel differently once this problem was solved.

The handful of cottages that made up the village were scattered rather than being neatly arranged in rows the way a larger town would be. There were six or seven of them lined up along the road, with the tavern farthest to the west, but the rest of the little buildings looked like a scattering of beads from a broken necklace, lying wherever someone had thought looked like a good place to build. Except for the tavern, which had a roof shingled with slate that must have come from far away, the cottages all looked the same: squarish or oblong construction, thatched roofs, small windows cut into the walls at random and covered with oiled paper. The spaces between the timbers of the frames were filled with wattle and daub, which meant the houses were at least fifty years old, probably older. Ginnevra had seen dozens of villages just like Arrus all over the Lordagne.

She smiled and nodded at the women gathered around the well, drawing water and gossiping as their children ran and screamed in play around them. Past the well, she waved at Damiano, who was busy at the forge. The hot, crisp smell of heated metal filled the air, a comforting smell that reminded Ginnevra of her childhood spent near her father's forge. A whiff of red-hot iron always carried her into the past.

She knocked on Agnella's door and got no response, so she walked around to the rear of the cottage and found the woman sitting near her garden, which was much larger and more fully grown than Ginnevra's. Agnella's needle flashed in and out of the shirt whose sleeve she was resetting. "My lady," she said with a cheerful smile. "You need more washing done?"

"If it's not too much trouble." Ginnevra waited for Agnella to put aside her mending before handing her the small bundle of cloth. Agnella's nose wrinkled.

"Hope you don't mind my saying, but that's a rank smell," she said.

"I must have walked through something nasty in the forest," Ginnevra lied. "Sorry."

"No, it's no trouble." Agnella's smile fell away. "You were in the forest? That's braver than I would be."

Ginnevra hooked the other chair with her foot and drew it nearer so she could sit comfortably close—close enough, she hoped, to invite confidences. "It *is* what paladins do," she said. "The villagers don't go into the forest?"

"Not since the monsters came." Agnella set Ginnevra's clothes on the ground far from her basket of mending. "Not much before that, neither. Nothing in that direction for a hundred miles."

"But surely there are things in the forest you need? Firewood, maybe?"

"That, yes, but we take from the tree line when we need to cut down a tree for aught." Agnella continued mending the shirt. "Though I suppose Ciecerella did go now and again to collect herbs."

"I don't think I've met Ciecerella." She hadn't met most of the villagers, so maybe that wasn't so surprising, but after her encounter with the dragon Ginnevra was inclined to suspicion.

Agnella smiled, a rueful expression. "She's sweet enough, but she keeps to herself most days. She's an herbalist and good with simples. Didn't she come to help you this last week, when you were laid up? Someone must have mentioned her to your brother."

Ginnevra had no idea what kind of relationship Eodan had developed with the villagers, but if they'd suggested he speak to this Ciecerella, he hadn't mentioned it to her. "He might have talked to her. He's an accomplished physician, but I'm sure he wouldn't have spurned any help that was offered. I'm afraid I was fairly ill for a while and don't remember much." She was talking too much, giving information Agnella didn't need out of a desire to conceal the truth. Quickly, she changed the subject, or at least redirected it. "I hope Ciecerella hasn't gone into the forest recently. I'm not sure all the monsters are gone."

"Yes, I heard tale as you mean to go deeper into the woods." Agnella shivered. She bit off her thread, folded the shirt, and picked up a pair of roughly woven wool hose with a tear down the inseam. "You think something's driving the monsters to us?"

Startled, Ginnevra said, "I—that's not what I said."

"Sorry, it was just a guess. It makes sense, though, doesn't it? Some bigger monster scaring away all the little ones, and they come upon Arrus...but then we'd have seen the bigger monster already, yes? Or was it that needle-toothed flying creature?"

"The maligna. Yes, I think so. But I have to hunt the forest to make sure there isn't anything else that might threaten your village." Ginnevra hated lying, even partially, to people who didn't deserve it, but even though she felt certain Agnella wasn't part of the dragon conspiracy, she couldn't tell her the truth until she knew who was.

"You should be careful," Agnella said. "You and your brother—he's a big one, isn't he? I wouldn't have guessed him to be a physician, but it takes all kinds, doesn't it?"

"People aren't always as they seem," Ginnevra said.

Armed with directions to Ciecerella's house, Ginnevra strolled on up the street and between houses until she came to one set a little farther back than the rest. It wasn't as secluded as hers was, but it was still distant enough to be noticeably separated. It also looked more rundown than the others, the walls grubby and patchy where bits of the mud daub had cracked and fallen away to reveal the woven framework within, the thatch sagging on one side. But brightly colored flowers bloomed in beds to either side of the door, filling the air with a sweet fragrance and giving the cottage a slightly less decrepit look.

Ginnevra knocked lightly on the door. No one answered. She knocked a little harder, looking around to see if there was anyone who might know if the herbalist was in. The nearby cottages were all quiet. "Hello?" she called out. "Ciecerella?"

The door cracked open, paused, then swung open fully. "Yes?" the woman behind it said. "You wanted to see me?"

"Are you Ciecerella?"

The woman nodded. She was small, petite and slender-framed, with long dark hair and a long face to match. Her nose was even beakier than Ginnevra's, and between that and her size she put Ginnevra in mind of a bird, one of the tiny ones that lived in the towers of the Citadel and dove after dropped bits of food in perfect, eerie silence. Like the birds, she said nothing, merely watched Ginnevra with wary eyes.

"I was hoping you could help me," Ginnevra said when it was clear Ciecerella wouldn't volunteer anything else. "I'm told you go into the forest frequently, or used to do, and I wondered if you'd gone recently."

Ciecerella wound a hand into her red apron, which was clean despite the old stains spattering it. "Why do you ask?"

"If the monsters truly are gone, the wildlife will return," Ginnevra said. "Have you noticed anything like that?"

Ciecerella shrugged. "I haven't gone back since Amabina was killed. I was scared to. That was over four weeks ago." She wouldn't meet Ginnevra's eyes, and her gaze darted restlessly in all directions, never settling for long on anything.

Amabina was the woman who'd owned Ginnevra's cottage. "What about before that?" Ginnevra pressed. "I'd like to establish what brought the monsters here, whether they were in the forest before the first attacks. Did you notice anything strange before that?"

"I don't know." Ciecerella still wouldn't look straight at Ginnevra. "I mostly only care about gathering herbs while I'm there. Never seen animals bigger than a squirrel or a jay. So I don't notice if the bigger ones aren't around."

Ginnevra hesitated. Ciecerella was acting suspiciously, but she might just be one of those people who was awkward around strangers or nervous about paladins. Her behavior didn't have to mean anything underhanded. But Ginnevra remembered how stupid she'd been not to pursue this inquiry sooner and decided to push a little harder. "That's all right," she said. "It was worth asking. I'm told you're good with healing herbs, is that right?"

For some reason, this startled Ciecerella into meeting Ginnevra's eyes. "I suppose," she said, warily.

"So when you go into the forest, is it to collect leaves and roots, or do you harvest entire plants for transplant?" Ginnevra had no idea where this line of conversation was going, and she hoped her instincts were leading her somewhere important.

"Something of both," Ciecerella said. Now she looked as if the strange paladin had gone mad, wanting to know about something so mundane as gardening.

"You know I'm caring for Amabina's house, right?" Ginnevra was struck by inspiration. "She had a lovely garden."

Ciecerella relaxed visibly. "She does. Did. Are you interested in gardening?" She asked the question as if sure the answer would be "no."

"I didn't think I was until I saw the garden plot there. I hope I'm caring for it properly. I'm not always sure of the difference between a vegetable and a weed." Ginnevra laughed, hoping she projected the right amount of hapless innocence. "I don't suppose you'd let me see your garden? I find I'm more interested now in what other people do with theirs."

Ciecerella nodded and came out of her cottage, shutting the door behind her. "Back here," she said.

Ginnevra followed her around behind the cottage and into the biggest garden plot she'd yet seen in Arrus. A tantalizing array of smells wafted from the myriad plants, spicy and sweet and even minty. "This must require so much work," she said, genuinely impressed.

"It's not so much if you keep up with the weeding daily," Ciecerella said. She sounded smugly proud. "This side's for food, and over here is my herb garden." She gestured, indicating an aisle wide enough for someone to comfortably kneel in, on either side of which grew luxuriously lush plants.

Ginnevra walked the aisle, looking at the greenery without recognizing more of it than the feathery tops of carrots. "I don't know what that is," she said, pointing at a plant at random.

"That's basil," Ciecerella said. She was back to sounding suspicious. "Don't know anyone doesn't recognize basil."

"I told you I'm not very experienced. It doesn't grow in my garden," Ginnevra improvised. "It can't be one of your healing herbs, though, yes?"

"Most herbs have healing properties if you know how to use them," Ciecerella said. "Basil's mostly for food, yes, but I make a tea from it that helps with women's monthlies. Not something a paladin needs."

"No, not really." One of the Dark Lady's blessings upon Her warriors was a remission of menses while they served Her. Ginnevra hadn't had a monthly bleeding in over five years and didn't miss it at all. "What about this? It looks like a common weed."

"It is a common weed, dock leaves." Ciecerella now had the expression of a schoolmistress about to deliver a lecture. "Only this is rhubarb. The leaves are for poultices, and the stalks are for stewing to eat. They're very tart and have to be mixed with honey."

"That's interesting, that you get so much out of one plant." Ginnevra shielded her eyes against the sun and looked out across the garden. "Did you grow the flowers, too?" Rows and rows of brightly-colored blossoms covered the otherwise fallow field past the garden.

"Those are for healing, too. Dandelions, and blue flags, and marigolds, all of them good for what ails a man." Ciecerella stopped at the edge of the garden and stood beside Ginnevra, looking at the flowers.

"I don't recognize the scarlet and white flowers," Ginnevra said.

"Lady-fair," Ciecerella said. She was back to sounding curt and withdrawn.

Ginnevra walked over to the nearest lady-fair. It was trumpet-shaped and bobbed on a long, fat green stem. "What are they good for?" She sniffed it, and to her surprise smelled nothing.

"They make a tea that's good for the complexion." Ciecerella turned and walked back toward the house. Clearly, the conversation was over. Ginnevra decided not to push the strange little woman further.

She followed Ciecerella back to the front door of the cottage. "I'm glad you haven't gone back to the forest," she said. "It's far too dangerous."

"That's why you're here, isn't it?" Ciecerella said. She shut the door definitively in Ginnevra's face.

Ginnevra walked back through the village, thinking about that encounter. She was sure, based on the pattern of Ciecerella's pauses and the occasional tenseness in her voice, that the woman had been in the forest much more recently than she'd claimed. That didn't make her complicit, but it did mean Ginnevra needed to keep an eye on her.

"My lady!"

It was Damiano. Ginnevra hadn't realized she'd reached the forge. She veered over to where the smith stood, a pair of tongs held in his hand as if he'd forgotten they were there. "My lady, how goes the search?"

"Well enough. You haven't been in the forest lately, have you?"

Damiano laughed. "Me, my lady? Not a chance. I stay well away from the place. Not sure it isn't haunted these days."

"You think so?" This was the first Ginnevra had heard it suggested that the dead of Arrus hadn't left for the Goddess's eternal reward. "Has anyone seen ghosts?"

"No." Damiano shook his head. "No, but with deaths like those, you'd expect ghosts, right? Do you know how to cast out a ghost, my lady?"

The memory of Nucca's shattered face rose up, striking Ginnevra an almost palpable blow to the chest. "It's...not easy," she said. "But don't worry. I haven't seen any evidence of ghosts in the forest."

"Oh, you haven't gone in there, have you?" Damiano's concern turned his usually jovial expression grave. "That's not safe."

"It's what I do, Damiano. And far better I find monsters there before they make their way out of the woods to Arrus, right?"

"I suppose so." Damiano didn't sound convinced. "You need that sword sharpened? Or re-silvered? On the house."

"I didn't know you had silvering," Ginnevra said.

"We live far enough out there's sometimes call for silvered weapons," Damiano replied. "Never can tell when werewolves might be a problem, and you paladins can't be everywhere at once." He jerked his elbow in the direction of the forge's back wall, where hung a knife with a long blade that gave off the telltale shimmer of a silver-coated weapon.

"Thank you," Ginnevra said. "My sword is fine now, but I'll bring it by when that becomes necessary."

She bade the smith farewell and headed back around the tilled fields to her cottage. A day ago, she would have passed that conversation off as normal. Now, her suspicious mind reviewed it carefully. Damiano might just have been expressing ordinary concern about her entering the forest, but he might as easily have had some sinister motive for keeping her away. No one else had suggested the possibility of ghosts, and that was the one monstrous creature even paladins were wary of. If he'd wanted to scare her off, ghosts might be a good deterrent.

She found Eodan outside the cottage, skinning rabbits. His hair was damp and he smelled less of the werewolf than usual. "Supper," he said. "What did you learn?"

"I'm not sure. I'm afraid everyone seems suspect now." She retrieved the other stool from inside the cottage and sat near him, watching him skin and clean the rabbits with neat strokes of her knife. "How much do you know about herbalism?"

"For healing? Enough. We make use of plants that grow wild rather than cultivating them. Why?" Eodan wiped the knife on a clean cloth, then wiped his hands.

"I think the village herbalist is hiding something. Did you talk to her at all while I was injured?"

"Is that Sesalla?"

"Ciecerella."

"That's the name. Maghinardo suggested she might have something I could use, but I never did track her down. Though I didn't try very hard. I was afraid anything I asked her for might give her a hint that you were wounded rather than ill, and I didn't want anyone wondering what had injured you." Eodan cleared away the offal and began stripping the meat from the bones. His hands moved quickly and deftly, making Ginnevra wonder, once again, what werewolf society was like. She hadn't expected him to know anything about cooking.

"Anyway, she went from being forthcoming to being completely withdrawn, but at random. I wondered—the thatch in the smokers was tainted with a soporific, yes? So we're looking for someone who has access to a substance like that, and who better than an herbalist?"

Eodan paused in cutting the meat into cubes. "It might not be something that grows in her garden. Though I haven't seen or scented any plants that would have that effect in the forest. Maybe I should take a look."

"Be careful," Ginnevra said, alarmed. "You're not exactly inconspicuous in either of your shapes."

"That's rich, coming from the champion of rushing into danger headlong," Eodan said with a grin. He swept the rabbit meat into the pot, which he'd already filled with water. "I'll go after dark, if you'll tell me which cottage."

"Easier to show you." The thought of going along on this venture relieved Ginnevra's mind. Eodan was stealthier than she was, and he'd be fine on his own, so she wasn't sure where the relief came from. She ignored the feeling, which had nothing to do with success or failure.

CHAPTER
TWELVE

When night came, she put on her dark red gambeson and led the way around the fields and the cottages, taking a wide path to the rear of Ciecerella's cottage. Eodan padded along beside her, an even darker shape than she was. Lights burned behind the windows of every home, and Ginnevra's acute hearing perceived snatches of conversation and the occasional laugh. It boded well that the people of Arrus could laugh. If they were still under siege, that would be unlikely.

She stopped well away from the expanse of wildflowers and sat in the ankle-high yellow grass. "It's just there," she told Eodan in a low voice. "She said the flowers are hers as well."

Eodan nodded and ran forward, disappearing among the tall blooms. Ginnevra glanced up at the sliver of moon, which was low on the western horizon. She wondered what the Goddess thought of her friendship with a werewolf. Why didn't the Dark Lady teach Her followers not all werewolves were evil? It didn't make sense that She was ignorant of their plight, even if She didn't care about them and believed it was right not to accept them into Her embrace. It made no sense. On the other hand, Ginnevra was just a paladin, not an anointed or a theologian, and maybe there were subtleties she would understand if she knew about them. She hoped she was doing the right thing. The thought of being shunned by her sister paladins for not having killed Eodan made her feel sick, almost as sick as the thought of killing Eodan did.

She listened carefully, but heard only the movement of grasses and plants swishing in the light wind. Its breezes carried the scents of smoke and roast mutton, of lavender and peppermint, and of Eodan's musk.

Then, close by, she heard a door open and shut. She knelt up to see past the garden and surveyed the dark landscape. A small figure, cloaked and hooded, appeared at the edge of the cottage. Ginnevra drew breath to whisper a warning, but Ciecerella didn't come into the garden. Instead, she hurried away eastward.

Ginnevra stood and took a few steps after her, then changed course and entered the garden, brushing aside the tall stems of the flowers and not treading very carefully. She found Eodan sniffing among the herb beds. "Come with me," she whispered, and hurried toward the front of Ciecerella's cottage, not waiting to see if he would follow.

Ciecerella had disappeared.

Ginnevra took a few more steps before coming to a halt. The woman hadn't been moving fast enough to pass beyond Ginnevra's range of vision, so she'd entered one of the cottages, but which one? Ginnevra didn't know the village or the villagers well enough to guess who Ciecerella might have had a nocturnal liaison with.

Eodan bumped her leg with his shoulder. "I guess it's nothing," she said, feeling disappointed. "Did you learn anything?"

Eodan turned away, retracing their steps. Ginnevra had expected him to share his knowledge immediately, and guessed that meant he hadn't learned anything. Doubly disappointed, she ran after him.

Eodan outpaced her, in part because she didn't try very hard to keep up, and was in human shape and dressed when she arrived at the cottage. "What was that about?" he asked.

"Ciecerella sneaked out of her cottage. I wasn't fast enough to see where she went."

"That's not good. She's not an innocent village healer," Eodan said. "She's got any number of potential poisons growing in her garden."

"I thought anything could be a poison if you ingest enough of it," Ginnevra said.

"That's true, but there are some poisons that aren't used for anything else, and she has most of them." Eodan sat, running his fingers through his hair in a restless motion Ginnevra now knew meant he was thinking hard. "And she has at least two herbs that can be distilled into a soporific, one of which is burned and inhaled."

"Which herb was that?"

"Those bloodroses. They look delicate, but just a few drops on a fire and you'll sleep like the dead for hours. I might have guessed that was what was in those smokers."

"You mean those white and red flowers? She said they were lady-fair."

Eodan sat up straight. "She told you that? Because that was a flat-out lie. There's no lady-fair in that garden."

They stared at each other. "She lied," Ginnevra said. "She wouldn't have done that if she hadn't suspected I know something."

"And it has to be that you know about the dragon, because why else lie about the one plant in that garden that could produce the effect we saw?" Eodan ruffled his hair back into a semblance of order. His beard was shorter than she remembered, as if he'd trimmed it that afternoon. "Either they guessed accurately, or that thing I sensed in the forest was one of our conspirators."

Ginnevra felt cold. "We might have a bigger problem," she said. "Suppose that person saw you change? If they know you're a werewolf—"

"They can't do anything with that knowledge unless they give themselves away, too," Eodan said. "Don't worry about me."

"But—"

"I've had a lifetime of hiding from humans, Ginnevra. I'm in no danger." Eodan's expression was grim. "Though you might be, if they know you associate with me. I can't imagine they'll take kindly to a paladin of the Goddess being friendly with a monster."

"I'm not worried about that." She was worried, a little, but it was unlikely any of these villagers could give her a real fight and even less likely one of them would send news of Ginnevra's unholy alliance to Abraciabene. "None of them will challenge me."

Eodan didn't look convinced, but he said, "Then we have to find out who Ciecerella met with tonight. How many villagers do you think are involved?"

"More than two, fewer than six," Ginnevra said. "More than that, and they wouldn't be able to keep it a secret. These little villages all know everyone's business. And fewer than that wouldn't have been able to contain the dragon while they set up the smoke trap."

"I don't know if it's better or worse that we're only looking for a few conspirators," Eodan said. "Even in a village this size, it might be hard to find them."

"I don't know what else we can do tonight." Ginnevra rose. "Short of knocking on every door until we find Ciecerella. Unless you can track her scent?"

"The smells of that garden masked any human scent, including yours, and I was right next to you," Eodan said. "We can go back into the woods tomorrow. They might have been spooked into going back there to make sure nothing's happened to the dragon." Eodan stood as well. "Maybe we'll get lucky, and I can track them."

"I hope so. Good night." Ginnevra pulled off her hood and unfastened her gambeson as she headed for the bedroom. At the door, she paused, struck by something she had never before considered: where did Eodan sleep? And in what form? She glanced over her shoulder, but he'd settled on the brick hearth with his back to the coals, removing his shoes, and wasn't looking her way. If he slept on the floor—guilt struck her, guilt and a sense of failed duty.

She almost asked him, but embarrassment and that uncomfortable feeling of guilt stopped her tongue. If he *was* sleeping on the floor, there wasn't anything she could do about it, since there was only one bed, and if she drew attention to that fact, it would only make her even more uncomfortable. It would probably discomfit him, too.

She closed the bedroom door between them and removed the rest of her clothes, then climbed into bed and ran through her usual relaxation routine, tensing and relaxing sets of muscles in turn from her toes to her shoulders. But sleep eluded her. Finally, she closed her eyes and told herself she *would* sleep, and fell into dreams of wading through seas of bloodroses that grew chin-high and gave off puffs of soporific black smoke that dragged her into deeper dreams she didn't remember come the morning.

Though she didn't remember them, her lingering dreams left her feeling as achy as if she'd overexerted herself the day before, and she ran through a stretching routine before dressing and leaving the bedroom. Eodan wasn't there. She helped herself to cheese and yesterday's bread and sat outside in the early morning sunshine to dispel what was left of her dreams. It was going to be another hot, beautiful day, without a single cloud in the azure sky. Ginnevra basked like a lizard in the sun and let herself forget, for a few moments, about monsters and dragons and villagers conspiring to capture a dragon hoard.

She heard Eodan approaching—by now his footsteps were instantly recognizable—and said, "Did you eat? I want to go into the forest before there's anyone around to see us enter."

"I've already been," Eodan said.

Her eyes flew open. Eodan looked tired, as if he'd slept as poorly as she had, and another thought of him sleeping on the floor flashed across her inner eye. "I thought you would wait for me," she said.

"I woke early and couldn't get back to sleep, so I thought I'd take

a quick look. No one's used the forest road since we were there last."
Eodan sat heavily beside Ginnevra and pinched the bridge of his
nose as if his head ached.

"Are you all right?" Ginnevra asked.

Eodan nodded. "I'm fine. Just tired. And I feel as if we're missing
something important."

"Like what?"

"I don't know. It's probably nothing. Just superstition." Eodan
sighed and stretched out his legs, longer than Ginnevra's and clad in
roughly-woven trousers rather than breeches.

"I think we should check on the dragon," she said. "If Ciecerella
told her partners what she suspects, that I know the truth, they
might have done something to...I don't know. Speed up their plan,
maybe? Or they might decide to cut their losses and kill it, though
I'm not sure how they'd manage that. Its hide looked incredibly
tough."

"If they did, they didn't use the forest road." Eodan stood. "Let
me get something to eat, and we can go."

Ginnevra nodded and hurried inside to put on her chainmail.
While she waited for Eodan to eat, she pondered the idea of killing a
dragon. Granted that usually it took a company to pin one down, a
dragon subdued the way this one was might be killable by a single
person. She'd heard dragons had weak spots in their hide, but not
where they were—the joints, she thought, because it would be too
much to expect a weak spot exactly over the heart. Maybe blunt force
was more effective, which made sense because of how its wing must
have been broken that way. If she—

—but this was foolishness, because she'd as much as promised
Eodan she wouldn't kill it. She couldn't remember how he'd maneu-
vered her into that promise. If it came down to a choice between the
life of the dragon and the life of an innocent human, she'd save the
human, no question. Aside from that, she had to admit she hadn't
felt a sense of menace from the dragon, not the way she did from
other monsters. Maybe Eodan was right, and the dragon was more

like a werewolf than, say, a maligna. It was worth looking into—so long as the thing didn't try to kill someone she was responsible for protecting.

Eodan emerged, biting into an apple. "Isn't it strange, eating fruit when a wolf is a carnivore?" she said.

Eodan looked at her and said nothing, just took another deliberate bite. Ginnevra felt stupid. "I'm sorry, that was rude," she said.

"Stranger if I ate raw meat in my human form," Eodan said, but there was a hint of anger beneath his calm words that made Ginnevra feel worse. She didn't need to draw attention to his unusual physiology and monstrous nature. Though he wasn't really a monster, not the way the term usually meant. She made herself stop thinking about it and controlled her embarrassment.

They strolled toward the forest's edge in silence. Ginnevra kept an eye out for watching villagers, but saw no one despite the sun being fully up. This time, the crunch and swish of dry grass beneath her boots didn't satisfy her; in fact, it made her irritable, as if she couldn't even walk silently as befitted a paladin of the Goddess. She kept her irritable thoughts to herself, not wanting to spread them to Eodan and make things even more awkward between them.

The quiet coolness of the forest was an unexpected relief, and Ginnevra, who loved the heat of the sun, was surprised at how much more comfortable she was when she was beneath its branches. Tiny patches of blue showed between the leaves, which trembled now and then in the wind that coursed across the canopy. The rustling sounded like whispers, or like water over stone, and it soothed Ginnevra's heart.

They reached the dragon's clearing, and Eodan, who hadn't changed shape, concealed himself near Ginnevra and said, "I don't think I realized how big it is before."

"I was actually thinking it's smaller than I imagined," Ginnevra said. "Either way, it's enormous by our standards." The dragon lay on its stomach, its legs curled beneath it and its unwounded wing draped over its back. The injured wing was folded beside it at an awkward angle. Now that she wasn't terrified, Ginnevra could appreciate the dragon's near-perfect camouflage, the thin green translucent membranes of its wings and the pattern of brown and gray and black and white that reminded her of a moth. It was surprisingly beautiful.

The bramble heaps lay unchanged, still emitting their sullen smoke. Ginnevra crossed the clearing to examine one more closely. "I wonder why it didn't put us to sleep? Or you, actually, since it's hard to poison a paladin."

"Werewolves in wolf shape are resistant to many poisons," Eodan said. "I don't dare get too close in this shape."

Ginnevra looked through the haze at the dragon's recumbent form. "I think you were right about their plan, or lack of it. If they keep it unconscious most of the time, it might not be strong enough to fly back to its hoard when its wing is healed."

"Which makes me wonder if they don't have another plan." Eodan walked the line of smokers, pacing slowly with his eyes fixed on the dragon.

Ginnevra followed him, wondering what he was looking for. Whether he still had fellow feeling for the creature, even though they were nothing alike—or was she wrong about that? They were both powerful, deadly creatures, terrifying to humans—and with that, she felt an unexpected rush of sympathy for Eodan and what it must be like to be neither human nor animal and feared by both.

"Eodan," she began.

Eodan held up a hand for silence. "I think it's awake," he whispered, but he didn't back away. Ginnevra searched the dragon for signs that it was stirring and at first saw nothing. Then it moved, ponderously slowly, and got to its feet.

Ginnevra held her breath, anticipating its next move. Between the smoke and the sleeping drug, she didn't think it could move fast enough to overpower either of them, but she readied herself to flee or fight. She thought about drawing her sword and decided against it. It might recognize a sword as a threat.

The wedge-shaped head lifted from the ground on the serpentine neck and shifted like it was scenting the air. The dragon took a few steps before sinking back to the ground, its legs shaking as if its weight was too much to support it. A puff of green smoke escaped its nostrils, wreathing its head in mist that softened its features.

Before she could stop herself, Ginnevra walked past the nearest bramble heap and approached the dragon. A sensible voice in the back of her head screamed at her to stop and think, but she was halfway to the dragon and it hadn't reacted yet, so she kept going. Behind her, Eodan swore viciously, and she heard the sound of him taking off his clothes. She ignored him for the moment, all her attention on the beast before her.

The dragon's eyes were half-lidded and milky white, she thought with nictitating eyelids rather than as a natural feature of its eyes, since they'd been yellow the last time she'd encountered it. But it was clearly watching her. She slowed her steps when she was within three feet of the monster and extended a hand, moving slowly and never looking away from its eyes. Still it regarded her with a lack of interest, blinking occasionally, little jets of green smoke spurting out with its rhythmic, deep breathing.

Then Eodan was at her side, pressing reassuringly close against her leg. "I think it's too stupefied to react," she murmured. With a final step, she rested her hand lightly on the dragon's flank.

It twitched, a full-body shudder that sent a ripple of force through Ginnevra's hand. Its mouth opened, and it croaked, the same sound it had made before. This time, it sounded weak, like that was the best it could manage. Then it sagged, closed its eyes, and fell asleep.

Ginnevra stood with her hand still on its rough hide. It was striated rather than pebbly or scaly as she'd expected, just like the bark it resembled, and even through her glove, it was warmer than her own skin. She let out a breath and waved her other hand in front of her face to dissipate the smoke that fogged her head and made her feel drowsy. "Let's get out of here," she said.

Once back beyond the line of smokers, Ginnevra waited for Eodan to resume his human shape before saying, "I don't know what I expected. I just...I think I wanted to touch it. To make it real rather than some mythical creature."

"I don't think I'll ever be used to how casually you risk your life," Eodan said. "Suppose it had torn you apart?"

"You saw how it moved. I doubt it had the agility to do anything like that." She turned to face Eodan, who looked ready to fight someone, possibly her. "There is something very wrong about all this. Those conspirators must be truly stupid not to see their plan won't work."

"Unless we're wrong about their plan," Eodan said. "But what else is there?"

"I don't know." Ginnevra sighed. "Let's check the path again, and the area around it. Not because I think you missed something," she assured him as he drew in a breath to protest, "but because I want to see if there's any way we can set an ambush for them."

"That might be difficult," Eodan said. "The trees don't grow thickly along the path, and there's not much in the way of undergrowth the closer you get to the village. But it's worth taking a look."

They made their way through the trees to the path, which still didn't look like more than a game trail. Ginnevra kept a close eye on the ground, but saw no tracks aside from those of a fox that crossed the path at one point. She wished idly that she had Ciecerella's knowledge of plants, to identify the ones she saw just out of curiosity. As it was, she knew the difference between a fern and poison ivy, neither of which she saw now.

Eodan, walking ahead of her, suddenly stopped. He lifted his head and sniffed. "Do you smell that?"

Ginnevra sniffed as well. The sweetish odor at first reminded her of the dragon's breath, but another sniff told her this was different, something ranker. Something that smelled of death.

Eodan took off through the undergrowth. Ginnevra followed him until he stopped again, this time so abruptly she ran into him and had to step back quickly. Eodan stood staring down at his feet. "Who is that?" he asked.

Ginnevra moved around him and froze. The body that lay before them was bloody from a dozen or more claw marks, but the woman's face was unmarked except for traces of blood along her chin. "Dear Goddess have mercy," Ginnevra said. "It's Ciecerella."

CHAPTER

THIRTEEN

E odan knelt beside the body. "This isn't good," he said, prodding her wounds with his fingers.

"That's an understatement. She's the only one we knew for certain was in on the dragon conspiracy." Ginnevra walked wide of Ciecerella and crouched on her opposite side.

"That's not what I mean." Eodan wiped his fingers on a nearby plant. "She wasn't killed by a monster. She was murdered."

"What?" Ginnevra stared at the body as if answers might spring from it. "But these are claw marks."

Eodan shook his head. "Take a look at this," he said, turning Ciecerella's head gently to one side. "She was killed by a blow to the head. The other wounds were inflicted later—there's not enough blood. And the edges are too clean, not torn. There aren't a lot of monsters with claws that sharp."

Ginnevra examined the wounds. "You're right. Only a maligna, or a werewolf—sorry."

"You're right, a werewolf could have done it," Eodan said with no trace of embarrassment. "But there's only one werewolf in the vicinity, and I know I didn't kill her."

"No." Ginnevra sat back on her heels. "Well, damn. Now what? Somebody killed her and tried to make it look like a monster attack. But we have no idea who."

"We have *some* idea," Eodan said. "It has to have been one of her fellow conspirators."

"But why?" The answer hit Ginnevra immediately. "They thought she was a risk because she talked to me."

"Do *not* blame yourself," Eodan said fiercely.

"I wouldn't. I don't. I'm looking at it from their perspective. If they were nervous before that I was poking around in the forest, me talking to Ciecerella might look like I'm closer to figuring out the truth than I actually am. If they thought she was a weakness...she wasn't forthcoming, but I think if I'd pressed her harder, she might have revealed more than she wanted." Ginnevra swore under her breath. "If I blame myself for anything, it's not doing just that. She might still be alive if I'd known to winkle the truth out of her."

"You don't know that. Focus on what we do next instead of dwelling on the past."

Ginnevra let out a long, slow breath and nodded. "All right. Someone was meant to find Ciecerella here in the forest and bring back reports of a monster who killed her. If I didn't know the truth, I'd go hunting. And we're back to them being stupid again, because me hunting in the forest is almost guaranteed to result in finding the dragon."

"Maybe not," Eodan said. "Suppose it was one of the conspirators who intended to find her? We don't know what they'd say about her death. They might have a story that would steer you down the wrong path."

"Which means we have to leave her here." Ginnevra rose and dusted off her hands, though they were clean of anything but a little dried blood. She felt grimy, unclean, and in need of a bath that would wash her spirit as well as her body. "We have to wait to see who 'finds' her, because that will be our next conspirator."

"It bothers me, too, leaving her here," Eodan said. "But this is the only way for her to receive justice."

Ginnevra stalked away through the undergrowth, wishing she had Ciecerella's killer in her hands. Life was precious and short and no one deserved for theirs to end so abruptly. She couldn't help remembering that small body back at the destroyed caravan that had, in a way, set all of this in motion. Sometimes there was no justice. There was just her, fumbling around like a blind woman with no idea of why or what any of this meant. She remembered what Eodan had said about feeling they were missing something. He was right; she felt it, too. But knowing that didn't make the missing piece spontaneously appear.

When they reached the cottage, Ginnevra washed her hands, wishing that were enough to cleanse her. She unstrapped her sword and leaned it against the front door. Then she sat on the bench outside the door and leaned against the wall, soaking in the sun with her eyes closed and her hands loosely gripping her knees. She felt Eodan sit beside her, but he said nothing, which was a comfort.

She wasn't sure how long they sat like that, waiting, before she heard shouting coming from the direction of the village. "This is it," she murmured. "Will you come with me?"

"If you want," Eodan said. "They know I'm a physician. It will make sense for me to examine the body. What should I say?"

"Tell them a maligna did it," Ginnevra said.

She rose to greet the child who came racing toward them and reflected on how similar this was to the day the squasc had been caught down the well. At least most of the monsters she faced were unequivocally evil and dangerous. She felt a moment's weariness at how ambiguous her life had turned out to be.

The child had to stop and gasp for breath before gabbling out his errand. Ginnevra had her sword on before he finished. "Let's go," she said.

The villagers were gathered around the community well, again like when the squasc had attacked. They parted for her and Eodan, and Ginnevra's throat closed up when she saw the wreck Ciecerella's body was in full daylight. "Where was she attacked?" she asked.

"I found her in the forest," one of the men said. "I knew she'd gone after herbs this morning, and I have an ailment, have had for a while now. It was something she harvested the cure for in the forest, and I thought as how I should let her know, so she didn't have to make another trip later." He was tall and darkly tanned, holding his flat cap in both hands and twisting it out of shape, and he wore a rather vacant, dull-eyed expression.

"What's your name?" Ginnevra asked.

"Tebaldo, my lady."

"Weren't you afraid of monsters?"

Tebaldo looked startled, as if she'd asked him to dance with her there on the commons. "Monsters? My lady, you've rid us of the monsters." He looked down at Ciecerella. "Or...I suppose..."

Ginnevra ground her back teeth in irritation. "Eodan?"

"It was a maligna," Eodan said from where he knelt beside the body. "Did anyone hear it? The same kind of creature that killed Stefano?"

Murmuring rose through the watching crowd. "I thought I heard something early this morning," said another man. This one was shorter, with thick, straight hair and a heavy beard. "I thought it was some kind of bird. You think it was that monster?"

Ginnevra examined him closely. "And you are..." She knew fewer of the villagers than she'd thought.

"Gasparo, my lady," the man said. Despite the beard concealing his face, he had an open, guileless expression that made Ginnevra instantly suspicious. Nobody looked that innocent unless they had something to hide. "I heard it coming from the south, near the forest."

"Anyone else?" Ginnevra asked.

A few hands lifted, timidly, as people began to say that yes, they'd heard a loud bird that morning, off to the south. Ginnevra saw the truth to Captain Attanante's frequent complaints that eyewit-nesses were less help than no witnesses at all. If not for the deadly seriousness of the situation, she might have laughed at how the villagers were quick to attest to her made-up story.

Finally, she said, "Tebaldo, I want you to take me to where you found the body. The rest of you, take care, and don't stray far from your homes. If the maligna is still nearby, you won't be safe."

She was out of the crowd with Tebaldo by her side when she realized Eodan had followed her. "What are you doing?" she whispered.

"You're not going into the forest alone with that man," Eodan whispered back.

Tebaldo had taken a few more steps ahead and was watching the two of them with the dull, unthinking placidity of a cow. Ginnevra eyed his thin frame and said, "You can't possibly think I'm in danger from someone like him. I could break him with my pinky finger."

"And suppose he has friends waiting to ambush you?"

Ginnevra rolled her eyes. "I'm not worried. And you can't come with me. It will look strange. Besides, you need to stay here to see if anyone else acts suspicious. I really doubt they're all in the forest to set a trap for me."

Eodan's lips thinned in irritation, pressed tight together like he was suppressing an outburst. "Fine," he said. "Someone has to care for the body, anyway."

"Thank you," Ginnevra said. "I promise to be careful."

Eodan raised his eyebrows, but said nothing.

Ginnevra kept a close eye on Tebaldo as they followed the path to the forest. He walked with his shoulders slumped and his head bowed, as if he didn't actually see his surroundings. Ginnevra had to remind herself she wasn't supposed to know where Ciecerella had been found and resist the urge to go running ahead.

When she wasn't watching Tebaldo, she watched her surround-ings. She hadn't lied to Eodan about not fearing an ambush, but she was well aware that it was best to plan for disaster so you weren't caught off guard by it. So she stayed alert, scanning the forest. Eodan was right; this would be a hard place to execute an ambush. At the moment, that benefited her.

Tebaldo led her directly to the spot Ciecerella had lain. "This is off the path, Tebaldo," Ginnevra said. "How did you know to look here?"

"There were flies," Tebaldo said. "I could tell something big had died here, and I thought...I don't remember what I thought. That I should see if it was a monster. I thought you might want to know." Then, to Ginnevra's utter astonishment, the man burst into tears.

She stared at him, thinking this might be a ploy to throw her off guard. It was working. "Um...are you...is something wrong?"

"She's dead," Tebaldo sobbed. "She was my sweetheart, and she's dead, and now all I can see when I think of her is—" He choked on a louder cry and covered his face with his hands.

Ginnevra again scanned the nearby forest. This could still be a trick, and Tebaldo's friends might leap on her while she was distracted. Nothing else moved. The forest was as unnaturally still as it always was. "She was your sweetheart?" she said.

Tebaldo nodded as if he couldn't manage words. Ginnevra listened for the sound of someone approaching and heard nothing over Tebaldo's weeping. Dread certainty welled up within her that this was no ruse.

She put a hand on Tebaldo's shoulder. "I'm so sorry. I wish you hadn't been the one to find her. No one should have to endure that." Rage began to supplant her dread. Those bastards had murdered a woman and then arranged for her lover to be the one who found the body. Ginnevra didn't care about justice. She was going to tear them apart.

"Tebaldo," she said, "this is important. I know you're grieving, but can I ask you some questions?"

Tebaldo raised his tear-ravaged face. "What kind of questions?"

"Were you telling the truth before about why you were looking for Ciecerella?" It hadn't sounded like the action of a lover.

But Tebaldo nodded. "It's how we fell in love. She's treated my ailment for months now. I know it probably doesn't seem romantic to you."

Ginnevra had very little experience with romance, so she didn't feel qualified to pass judgment. "So you went to her house this morning—"

Tebaldo shook his head. "No, I was going to, but Gasparo said he'd seen her headed for the forest. So I just followed her." Tears welled up in his eyes again.

"Gasparo?" Ginnevra's suspicions reared their heads again. Gasparo had sent Tebaldo on his grisly mission. And he'd been the first to claim he'd heard a maligna in the forest, in a direction away from the path and the dragon. "Did he mention having heard a monster earlier?"

"No, my lady." Tebaldo wiped his eyes with his sleeve. "I would have gone faster if I'd known that. I might have saved Ciecerella—" His voice cut off again.

"You can't think like that," Ginnevra said, gripping his shoulder. "It's blasphemous to believe you know what outcome would be best, as if it was destiny. For all you know, if you'd left earlier you would have shared Ciecerella's fate. Do you think she wants you dead?"

Tebaldo's eyes were wide. "Of course not," he whispered, "but—"

"But, nothing. We embrace what comes, even if it hurts, and choose our path as it unfurls before us. The Goddess doesn't tell us our future because She wants us to be free to choose. Mourn Ciecerella's loss, but don't let it blind you to what is."

"I see." Tebaldo wiped his eyes again. "Thank you, my lady. But I don't think I'll ever stop mourning her."

"There's nothing wrong with mourning if it makes you a better man." Ginnevra released him. "Thank you, Tebaldo. I'm sorry for your loss. And I promise to make sure no one else in the village suffers Ciecerella's fate."

It would be an easier promise to keep than Tebaldo realized,

Ginnevra reflected as they returned to Arrus. If Gasparo was one of the conspirators, and she was sure he was, Ginnevra intended to twist him until he broke and revealed all. And then she would see him and the others hang for murder. She felt full of hot, satisfying anger she tamped down until it simmered. Anger under control was a weapon. Anger unchecked was a weapon aimed at one's own heart.

The crowd had dispersed when they returned. Eodan and the body were also gone. Ginnevra thought about asking where he'd gone, but decided she needed to collar Gasparo first. "Where does Gasparo live?" she asked Tebaldo.

Tebaldo gave her another dull-eyed look that said he was back to grieving again. "His house is back that way, but he's likely to be working at this hour. He's the butcher."

Ginnevra hadn't realized Arrus was big enough to have a butcher, but as she thought back on the last week or so, she remembered Eodan coming back with meat he couldn't have skinned and butchered himself. "Where is that?"

Tebaldo pointed. "Back away to where the stink won't bother none." He turned and slouched away. Ginnevra felt another pang of sorrow for him she turned into simmering anger.

She strode through the scattered cottages, not acknowledging the few people she passed. At this time of day, almost everyone was at their work, either tending the fields or doing household chores, though Ginnevra suspected most of the villagers would find excuses to gather and gossip about Ciecerella's death. She hoped that didn't include Gasparo. It would be easier to wring the truth out of him if he was alone.

She smelled raw meat and blood long before she saw the...you couldn't really call it an abattoir, not on this small a scale, but it was definitely where animals were slaughtered. Ginnevra still didn't know why Arrus rated a full-time butcher, but that was one mystery she didn't have to unravel.

Gasparo, wielding a long knife, was stripping the skin from a cow carcass hanging from a hook in the ceiling. He glanced Ginnevra's way, nodded politely, and said, "Do you need aught, my lady?"

"Just a moment of your time, Gasparo. I have some questions."

"If you don't mind waiting, I just need to finish this." With a few more deft strokes, he loosed the skin from the body. He thrust the knife into his belt without cleaning it and tugged the skin free. It was an expert job, and despite herself Ginnevra admired his skill.

"I'm surprised there's enough need for a butcher's services," she said, deciding to pretend to amiability for now. "I thought people in Arrus killed their own animals."

"Most do," Gasparo said. "But the bigger animals, pigs and cows and the like, some people can't handle the butchering efficiently. So when that's necessary, I skin and clean and butcher for a fee, and tan the leather."

"I haven't seen herds of cows in the area."

"We have a small herd south of here. Belongs to the village, a gift from my lady, the Principessa, years ago. Bandono and Cholla have the keeping of it. This one—" He jabbed a thumb at the hanging carcass— "came down sick with something, and Bandono didn't want it spreading to the herd, so we culled her."

Ginnevra nodded. "So the meat will go to everyone?"

"Indeed. But you didn't come here to talk about cows." Gasparo wiped his hands on a stained cloth that he tucked into his belt next to the knife.

"I'd like you to tell me more about the creature you heard," Ginnevra said. She took a few steps to the side, away from a table stained dark with old blood, so nothing stood between her and Gasparo.

Gasparo didn't seem to notice that she was gearing up for a fight. "It's like I said earlier. I thought it was a bird. Maybe a sick bird, the way it was crying. It was a terrifying sound, and I'm glad it wasn't anywhere near here."

"And was this before or after you saw Ciecerella heading to the forest?"

Gasparo looked thoughtful. "After," he finally said. "Not more than an hour after."

"That doesn't sound like much time for it to kill Ciecerella and then move that far south," Ginnevra said.

Gasparo shrugged. "I'm not an expert on monsters. Was there anything else? Only I need to get to cutting this beast up."

Ginnevra's gaze drifted to the ceiling. Several heavy iron hooks hung there in addition to the one supporting the carcass. "Those look sharp."

Gasparo looked briefly confused. "I guess they are."

"Sharp enough to tear flesh? Human flesh?"

"They could, but I don't understand you, my lady." Gasparo didn't look confused anymore. He looked impassive, like his expression concealed some other reaction.

Ginnevra changed tactics. "Why did you send Tebaldo into the forest after Ciecerella?"

Gasparo blinked. "I didn't. I just told him I'd seen her going that way."

"And did you know they were sweethearts?"

"Of course," Gasparo said. "Everyone knew."

Ginnevra tamped down on a surge of rage. "I wish you hadn't said that," she said. "I'd hoped it was an accident that you'd put Tebaldo in a position to discover her body."

Gasparo put on a look of confusion so perfect it couldn't be real. "I don't understand. You make it sound like I knew Ciecerella was dead."

Ginnevra regarded him with a cold, flat stare and said nothing.

The man took a step back and bumped into the carcass, sending it swinging slightly. "Just what are you accusing me of, my lady?"

"I don't know if you killed Ciecerella, or if you just helped cover up the murder," Ginnevra said, taking a single step forward. She pointed at the meat hooks. "Those would leave marks just like a monster's claws, wouldn't they? So I'm certain you had *something* to do with it. Tell me who you were working with."

Gasparo's eyes were wide and fixed on Ginnevra's. "You can't prove anything."

"The Goddess grants us Her shelter in keeping our business private," Ginnevra said, "but She has no compassion for those who use Her gift to commit crimes. It is Her servants' duty to bring those secrets to light. I will keep asking questions, Gasparo, until the truth is known, and when that happens, if you've obstructed me in any way, the justicers will take that into account. Not in a good way. So I suggest you tell me the truth, now."

Gasparo stepped away from the carcass, suddenly calm. "Bring secrets to light? That's rich, coming from you."

His abrupt change in demeanor startled Ginnevra, but she concealed her surprise and said, "This isn't helping you, Gasparo."

"You've got secrets, too," Gasparo said with a smile that made him look like a predator. "Secrets I'm sure you don't want revealed. How safe do you think you and your so-called brother will be if I tell the village what he really is?"

It felt like a blow to the chest, stunning Ginnevra. "I don't know what you think you know," she managed, "but no one will believe your lies."

"They won't have to." Gasparo's smile widened. "You're so friendly with the monster, you aren't likely to do your duty. But I've a friend who's on his way to take care of him right now."

It was Ginnevra's turn to be confused. "What are you talking about?"

"Silvered blade, that's what it takes, right?" Gasparo chuckled. "The werewolf won't know to suspect him, and one good thrust is all it takes if you've got the right knife."

"But no one here—"

In a flash, Ginnevra remembered the silvered knife hanging on Damiano's forge wall. Her breath caught. "He wouldn't," she whispered.

"We're just simple peasant folk, not like you, high-and-mighty lady," Gasparo said. "We kill evil when we see it. We don't let it sleep in our bed. Tell my secret, and I'll raise the village against you. After we—"

Ginnevra punched him so hard she heard a rib crack. Gasparo cried out and fell backward. "I'll be back," Ginnevra snarled, "and we'll see which of us survives our secret being told." She whirled and sprinted for her cottage.

CHAPTER

FOURTEEN

S he dashed through the stupid maze of cottages, cursing silently, and stumbled to a halt at the forge. It was empty, the forge unlit. Ginnevra searched the wall. The silvered blade was missing. Her heart in her throat, Ginnevra ran on.

Panicked thoughts gibbered in the back of her mind. Common sense tried to calm them. Eodan was strong, too strong to be overpowered by a human, even one as well-muscled as Damiano. Her fear was unfounded. But she couldn't help picturing Eodan opening the cottage door, Damiano pretending to innocence, then a blade buried deep in Eodan's stomach or chest. He wouldn't know to guard against treachery, and it would get him killed.

She pushed herself faster than she had ever run before, her sword banging against her shoulder, driving her mad. It didn't slow her down, and that was all that mattered.

Time seemed to slow until she felt she was running through warm honey, heated to liquid by the late afternoon sun. Sweat prickled beneath her arms and down her back, but the normally pleasant feeling of physical exertion only made her feel ill with how slowly she was running. If she was too late, she didn't care if it wasn't strictly justice, she was going to take Damiano's head off and then go back for Gasparo's.

She plowed straight through the tilled fields, ignoring the cries of protest from the farmers. They could replant. Ahead, her cottage stood, looking perfectly peaceful in the bright sunlight, the garden emitting the smell of healthy green growing things that made her want even more to vomit.

She sped up the slight rise leading to the cottage and saw, in one heart-stopping moment, the door hanging slightly ajar. Fear gave her one final burst of speed, and she slammed the door open, shouting, "*Eodan!*"

Eodan looked up from the table. A basket of pea pods sat in front of him, along with a bowl half-full of shelled peas. He was alone in the front room. "What's wrong?" he asked, then, "You look terrified. Did something happen?"

Ginnevra's chest heaved as her lungs tried to compensate for the demands she'd put on them. "Where's Damiano?"

Eodan's puzzlement deepened. "Why would he be here? I haven't seen anyone since I left Ciecerella's body to be prepared for burial."

"He's going to kill you," Ginnevra panted. "He has a knife, a silvered knife—Gasparo knows what you are—they threatened to tell everyone, right after they killed you—"

Eodan pushed his stool back and stood. "Nobody's going to kill me," he said. "Certainly not a couple of peasants who think a silvered knife is enough. Calm down, Ginnevra."

Ginnevra shook her head. Her body quivered as her exertions caught up with her. "You're right," she said. "I don't know what I was thinking." She let the sword in its sheath fall to the ground, too tired to stop it.

Eodan came toward her. "You were really worried," he said, sounding amused. "I don't know what to say. I didn't think you could be so afraid for a monster's safety."

Ginnevra looked at him, at his wry smile and the amusement in those odd blue eyes, and her heart gave a little sideways lurch. "You're not a monster," she whispered.

Eodan's smile fell away. He looked at her curiously, as if she were a mystery he didn't know how to begin to solve. Then, hesitantly, he reached out and slid his hand gently along the curve of her cheek.

She couldn't remember him ever touching her before, and if he had, it certainly hadn't felt like this. His skin was rough and warm, almost hot, and his touch was light and sent a different kind of shiver through her. She stared at him, her mind a white blank. He looked like he was waiting for a response, but she couldn't remember how to speak or move. Her awareness of the cottage, of the table and the bowl of peas and the hearth and the one window, all faded to nothing. It was just the two of them, facing each other across an unfathomable gulf bridged only by his hand on her face.

She realized they were standing very close together, and she couldn't remember how they'd gotten that way, whether he'd come to her or she'd gone to him. All she knew was that he was close enough for her to hear his breathing, deep and slow, and more faintly the rhythm of his beating heart.

His hand shifted again, and without thinking, she raised her own hand to cover his much bigger one. With an almost imperceptible pressure, he tilted her head back slightly, took another step toward her, and kissed her.

His lips were warmer even than his hand, warm and gentle as she would never have expected from a man his size. She kissed him back, enjoying the rush of pleasure that flooded through her. It had been a long time since she'd kissed a man, but abstinence couldn't explain this wonderful sense of excitement she felt from his touch, how she longed for him to take her in his arms and hold her close.

She took hold of the front of his shirt, pulled him closer, and felt his arm shift along her side. He let out a gasp of pain and jerked away abruptly. Ginnevra, surprised and hurt at his reaction, opened her eyes and saw an angry red welt forming along the inside of his wrist, right where his arm had brushed her side.

No. Where his arm had touched her silvered mail.

Ginnevra backed away, horror supplanting desire. She hadn't thought beyond kissing Eodan, and she'd forgotten everything else. What he was. What *she* was.

A chorus of voices rang in her head. *Werewolf. Monster. We kill his kind,* said her sister paladins. *You have a duty,* Captain Attanante said. *The Goddess gave you a gift, and you spurn it,* the Blessed said. Ginnevra put her hands over her ears like a child trying to block out a thunderstorm, but the voices wouldn't stop. *He's not a monster,* she silently cried, but she knew regardless of what she felt, regardless of what she knew, he *was* a monster so far as everyone she cared about believed.

So far as her oaths went.

She felt sick and dizzy and so confused she wasn't sure where she was or how she'd gotten there. With a cry of anguish, she turned her back on Eodan and flung herself out the door. She heard him shout something, but she was already running for the distant tree line, tears blinding her so she saw the forest as a series of blurs, dark brown shading to lighter brown and then to a muddled mass of green.

She ran without thinking until she passed beneath the trees, then kept going, crashing through the undergrowth. She didn't know how long she'd run before she tripped over an exposed root and fell to her knees, once more breathing so heavily her ribs hurt. She knelt there, listening, but heard nothing but the stillness of the forest. Eodan hadn't followed her, for which she was grateful. He could have outpaced her if he'd tried, and she couldn't bear to look at him.

She bent double until her head touched the ground, still kneeling, and didn't try to stop the tears from falling. Her mind flitted from thought to thought, never settling anywhere. He was a monster. He wasn't a monster. He was what she was sworn to kill. He was gentle and kind and nothing like she'd ever imagined a werewolf could be. Her duty was clear. Her duty made no sense. And, at the core of the whirlwind, lay the single stark realization that she had fallen in love and it was likely to break her heart.

Now that she was alone, she could remember what hadn't registered at the time: Eodan's face, his eyes wide and his jaw slack in uncomprehending pain, not from the silver but from Ginnevra's rejection. She groaned and beat her fists against the ground. She was so stupid not to have seen this coming. He looked like a man—a very attractive man—but he wasn't human, and she had no business falling in love with him.

She threw her head back and screamed out her confusion and pain. Her oaths were clear; she was sworn to hunt and kill the monsters who preyed on humanity. But Eodan wasn't a monster, not in that way. He didn't kill humans. So didn't that make him different, and not someone she was duty-bound to destroy? Or was she simply trying to justify having what she wanted?

No. She'd known he was different almost from the beginning. And she couldn't bring herself to believe there was anything wrong with her desire for him. It wasn't like he was an animal. But she wasn't sure the distinction would matter to the Blessed or to the other paladins. As far as they were concerned, werewolves were evil, and falling in love with one was dangerous or deviant or both.

Ginnevra curled in on herself. "Dark Lady," she prayed aloud, "I don't understand this path I'm on. I know You did not intend a destiny for me, and I don't want to know the future. I just need to know if I'm wrong to feel this way. He's not a monster, Goddess, I know he's not! And if he's not, then why should I not love him? But I can't...I can't bear the thought of losing Your grace. And I don't know what to do."

With a rush like wings on the air, a great wind roared through the upper canopy, filling the air with sound. Ginnevra shielded her eyes and looked up at where the branches tossed and the blue sky was visible as fractured shards of azure glass. She felt unexpectedly cold, as if the wind had come from the heart of a northern glacier, and reflexively touched her grace. It burned against her fingers, and she jerked them away with a hiss of pain.

But the heat didn't scorch her throat. Instead, warmth spread from the black pearl up her neck and down her chest and across her shoulders, flowing steadily until she no longer felt cold. Ginnevra shifted to sit rather than kneel and continued to watch the trees dance. Peace filled her heart. She didn't know what it meant, though she didn't think it was an answer, just a reassurance that she was not outcast, not yet.

She wrapped her arms around her knees and the chainmail pressed against her chest. She'd hurt Eodan, physically and emotionally, and her heart ached to know it. He didn't deserve to be...not led on, exactly, but she had kissed him and given him the impression she wanted him to kiss her. And now she didn't know what he thought. That she'd spurned him, naturally, but did he understand why? Probably not, since she wasn't sure she understood it herself.

She rested her cheek against her knees, feeling not the rough pressure of her breeches but Eodan's hand on her face. She couldn't understand how she could have fallen in love with someone she'd started out hating and wanting to kill. Maybe she was deviant. But she couldn't believe that. He was good and kind and patient and there was no reason she shouldn't have come to appreciate those qualities. Appreciate, and so much more.

Her body stirred with the memory of kissing him. She hadn't even remembered that he wasn't human until later, and maybe that meant something. Maybe it meant his race didn't matter. Or it could mean she was right, and werewolves weren't inherently evil. On the other hand, it might just mean she was ruled by her passions, but she never had been before, part of why it had been so long since she'd been with a man.

Impatience flashed through her, impatience with herself and her diffidence. Paladins didn't wait around for the Goddess to tell them what to do. They took action and did their best to live their oaths. Well, as far as Ginnevra was concerned, her oath was not to blindly murder creatures just because they had a bad reputation. She was supposed to kill actual monsters. And Eodan was not a monster. He was who she loved, and she defied anyone to tell her she was wrong.

Immediately, she felt a pang of guilt. Nobody would understand this, least of all her sister paladins. She was in for a long, long series of battles, possibly literal ones. She quashed her fear ruthlessly. If she was right about werewolves not being monsters, she needed to have the courage of her convictions. That would be true no matter who she loved.

She rose, dusted herself off, and slowly made her way back to the cottage. She had no idea what she would say to Eodan. Apologize, of course, but now that she'd made her decision, she wondered if it would matter to him. She might have hurt him more than he could bear. The thought made *her* heart hurt. She couldn't stop remembering how devastated he'd looked and remembering how he'd kissed her, like he'd put his whole heart into it. And she'd turned from him and fled. That didn't bode well for a future together.

That made her wonder what kind of a future they might have together. She was still a paladin, and she would have to return to her company sometime. Some paladins had long-term romantic relationships with non-paladins, and it was complicated enough without the non-paladin being a werewolf. Or...

A chill ran through her. Suppose he didn't *want* a future with her? Suppose she was mistaken, and his kiss had meant only that he was attracted to her and wanted a night or two in her bed? Ginnevra felt sick again. She breathed deeply until the feeling passed. One thing at a time. First, apologize, and make things as right as she could. Everything else could wait.

Her steps sped up when she was within sight of the cottage. She hated leaving things in limbo and always preferred talking out a problem immediately, no dithering or waiting around. Quickly, she pushed open the cottage door.

Eodan was gone.

She checked her bedroom, though she didn't know why he

would be in there, and then sat at the table. The bowls of pea pods and peas were still there. She picked at the seam of a pod until it cracked open, then ate the peas revealed. She couldn't think where he might go.

She remembered Damiano and his knife then, but the fear that struck her was less this time. Eodan was right; he wouldn't stand there and let Damiano stab him, especially now that he knew Damiano was one of the conspirators. That reminded Ginnevra of Gasparo. He'd probably lied to her about Damiano's intentions so he could escape. She ought to round him and Damiano up, though she didn't know where she could confine them. She should send to the nearest city for a justicer to try and convict them...but she needed to worry about their plan for the dragon...oh, there was just too much to deal with all at once. Time to make a real plan.

So, what did she know? She knew Gasparo had at least been part of Ciecerella's murder, or at any rate had helped cover it up. She knew Gasparo had seen Eodan change at some point to know he was a werewolf. He might have been the one Eodan had seen but not caught in the forest. And she knew Damiano was Gasparo's co-conspirator and that he, too, knew Eodan was a werewolf. The immediate question was, how badly did Ginnevra need to keep Eodan's secret?

Ginnevra ate more peas. They were little bursts of green on her tongue, delicious and sweet. It came down to whether the villagers would believe Gasparo and Damiano over a paladin. And if the paladin accused the two men of murder, well, that could go either way. The rest of the villagers might turn on the two, or they might turn on Ginnevra. Since she wasn't going to keep Gasparo and Damiano's crime a secret, it didn't matter what the villagers did. Which further meant Ginnevra wasn't going to give in to blackmail, and if Gasparo revealed Eodan's secret, they'd just have to endure.

She still didn't know what the two villains had planned for the dragon. That seemed like a less urgent problem than the question of how to confine them pending trial, but it was still important. It was something she could wring out of them once they were properly contained.

The door opened, startling Ginnevra. Eodan entered and stopped a few paces in. He looked as closed-off and emotionless as she remembered him being when they'd first met. In the face of that expression, Ginnevra's intent to apologize died. "Are you...where did you go?" she faltered.

"Out," Eodan said. "I looked for Damiano, but no one had seen him. Nor Gasparo."

"Oh." That might be a problem, but she had a bigger one right in front of her. She swallowed the lump in her throat and said, "Eodan. About—"

"I don't want to talk about it," Eodan said flatly. "We should try the forest. They may have gone to ground there."

"Oh," Ginnevra said again. Her heart pounded, insisting she not accept his refusal to talk. This wasn't going away, and if they didn't talk about it—on the other hand, he was the injured party, and maybe it was wrong for her to insist on talking and possibly hurting him more. She would wait, and eventually he would be ready. She hoped.

"Maybe we should wait until nightfall, so you can track them more easily," she added. "Unless you think finding them is urgent. It's only one or two more hours."

Eodan shrugged. "You're the paladin. It's your call."

Ginnevra felt as if he'd slapped her. For a moment, anger over-rode her pain. Then she came to her senses. He had every right to be upset, and lashing out was natural. That didn't make it easier for her to accept.

"I don't think Damiano or Gasparo will leave Arrus. Their whole lives are here," she said. "Can you track them in that shape?"

"Not as easily." Eodan shrugged again. "We have an advantage in darkness, anyway. We can wait."

Ginnevra nodded, but inside she felt like weeping. She wasn't sure she could stand a few hours of this taut non-communication.

She clung to how grateful she was that he hadn't just left forever and added, "Gasparo as much as admitted to complicity in Ciecerella's death, and he implicated Damiano. I don't have any idea how to contain either of them until a justicer arrives."

"There has to be an unused cottage somewhere." Eodan still sounded distant and angry, but at least he was talking to her. "Guards might be more of a problem. These people might be sympathetic to their own, even if their own murdered another villager."

"Let's track them down and worry about the rest later," Ginnevra suggested.

Eodan sat and pulled the bowl of pea pods toward himself. "There might be more ripe vegetables in the garden. You should take a look."

Ginnevra knew a dismissal when she heard it. Blinking back tears, she headed for the door.

CHAPTER
FIFTEEN

J ust after sunset, Ginnevra retrieved her sword and shrugged the belt on. Dinner had been as awkward and silent as the rest of the afternoon, making Ginnevra wonder why Eodan was still there. If he felt some kind of responsibility to this mystery, she didn't know why. It wasn't as if it had anything to do with him. She was starting to feel angry about his ongoing coldness. If he didn't care anything about her, if he was going to hang on to his resentment, he could do that just as easily a hundred miles away.

She loaded her pistol and shoved it angrily into its case at her waist. She hoped she wouldn't need it. It seemed like such a waste of silver to use it on a human. She remembered the welt on Eodan's wrist and closed her eyes to shut the memory away. The longer they persisted in silence, the less likely it seemed that they would ever return to where they'd been that morning.

Eodan had changed to his wolf shape while Ginnevra was arming up, and they walked to the village in a strained, uncomfortable silence Ginnevra longed to fill with words: *I'm sorry, I was wrong, I love you.* But she wasn't going to impose on him, especially not while he was in a shape that couldn't answer back.

Instead, she considered her options. She really needed to question Damiano before accusing him in front of the village. There was still a chance—a very slim chance—Gasparo was lying, and Damiano had nothing to do with any of this. But Ginnevra remembered the missing knife, and she was sure that wasn't the case.

Unless Damiano had left Arrus entirely, which seemed unlikely, he was somewhere in the area. Tracking him from the forge was dangerous, even though the villagers usually retired early and didn't venture out into the darkness, but it was their best chance of locating him.

When they reached the road through the village, Ginnevra gestured to Eodan to stay back while she checked for movement. Lights were on in most of the cottages, but the forge was dark and so was the house next to it. Eodan slunk into the depths of the forge, where he disappeared into the darkness. Ginnevra strode up to the house and knocked on the door. No response. She banged harder and said, "Damiano! Open up!"

Her keen hearing picked up movement in the cottage across the road a moment before that door opened and Maghinardo said, "Damiano's gone, my lady. He went hunting this afternoon, and he's usually gone for a few days when he does that."

"Thank you," Ginnevra said.

"Was it urgent business, my lady?"

Ginnevra regarded Maghinardo, who had no idea the trouble she was about to bring down upon him and his neighbors. "It will keep," she said.

She waited for Maghinardo to retreat safely inside his home before returning to the forge. Eodan had changed back to human form and was crouched where he wasn't more than a dim shape even to Ginnevra's eyes. "Damiano's scent is all over the place, but there are two tracks leading away from here, east and west. I think we should try the forest first."

Ginnevra nodded. She waited for Eodan to resume his wolf shape and then trotted behind him as he loped toward the forest. West meant away from Arrus, toward civilization. She might be wrong about Damiano's disinclination to flee. In that case, Gasparo might not know he'd been left hanging. A worry for another time. First, they needed to catch Damiano, and if they were very lucky, they'd find Gasparo with him.

Eodan slowed his pace once he entered the woods. Beneath the trees, the world was dim and formless, with tree trunks stark lines against the backdrop of dark green bushes and foliage. The path wound through the forest as aimlessly as ever, barely visible against the undergrowth. Ginnevra still heard no night birds, no rustling of leaves to show the passage of deer or foxes. There was only the soft wind in the branches above, occasionally gusting hard enough to make the topmost branches flail, and the sound of a million insects blending into a high, whining noise Ginnevra occasionally became aware of. She'd never seen anything so eerie.

She followed Eodan, who kept his head low to the ground. She had expected Damiano's path to diverge from the beaten track, especially if he knew Eodan was a werewolf and capable of tracking by scent, but it stayed right with the trail for several minutes. Finally Eodan stopped and gestured with his head in a northeasterly direction. Ginnevra looked and saw the trees thinning out in that direction. The dragon's clearing.

She nodded to indicate understanding, and Eodan moved off toward the clearing, more slowly now. Ginnevra crouched to alter her silhouette, though she didn't think Damiano's night vision was good enough to perceive her no matter how she walked. As she walked, she listened for anything that might reveal the presence of others. She heard nothing at first, not even the insects, whose drone had become so omnipresent her brain ignored it. Then, very distantly, she heard a murmur, the sound of two people talking. Lights gleamed within the clearing, torches rather than lanterns, barely more than a glimmer from where she stood.

She put a hand on Eodan's ruff to stop him and crouched beside him to whisper into his ear. "Two men arguing. You need to stay back—"

Eodan's lips curled in a silent snarl.

"I need you to sneak around to the north side of the clearing, get behind them for an ambush. I'll see if I can't work them around to put their backs to you. Don't worry. There are just two of them, right?"

Eodan fixed her with his blue-eyed gaze. Impulsively, Ginnevra put a hand on his head and said, "It will be all right. Thank you for worrying about me." Then she turned and, without waiting for him to go, walked into the clearing.

Immediately, she realized her mistake. There were four men, not two—three men and a woman, in fact—but one of the men and the woman were totally silent, watching the argument between Damiano and Gasparo. The torches lit the men's faces, giving them a monstrous appearance. She kept walking without hesitation, not wanting them to think she was afraid. Four or two, none of them were trained warriors, and none of them were a challenge to her skills.

Gasparo had his back to her, but Damiano saw her coming and shut his mouth. "What?" Gasparo said irritably, turning. He froze. Ginnevra walked until she was within ten feet of the little group, then stood with her arms crossed over her chest. Beyond them, the line of smokers continued to send up gray clouds that drifted eastward, and beyond that, the dragon lay still, sprawled in sleep or unconsciousness.

Gasparo spoke first. "So you've found us," he said, not sounding the least bit afraid or respectful. "I suppose your hairy friend is responsible? Where is he, anyway?"

"You should be worried about me, Gasparo," Ginnevra said. "I am the Goddess's representative, with power to arrest you and take you in for trial. Whatever you four are up to, I intend to stop it."

"Trial?" the unfamiliar man said. He took a step toward Gasparo. "Trial, why? We've done nothing wrong."

"Shut up, Baldo," Gasparo said without turning around. "You've no proof," he said to Ginnevra. "Nothing but guesses and empty threats. I suggest you leave Arrus before we raise the village against you."

"How well do you think that will work when they know what you did to Ciecerella?" Ginnevra shot back. "What do you think will matter more to them—allegations of a monster in their midst, or the knowledge that you murdered an innocent woman?" Innocent probably didn't describe Ciecerella, since she'd been one of the conspirators, but she hadn't deserved murder.

"What is she saying?" the woman said, glancing at Baldo and then back at Gasparo. "Ciecerella was killed by that monster, or one of them."

"It's a lie, Mella," Gasparo said, again without taking his eyes off Ginnevra. "She's trying to make you doubt. Don't listen to her."

"So not all of you were in on it," Ginnevra said. She looked at each of them in turn. Baldo and Mella looked genuinely confused. Damiano was scanning the clearing, possibly looking for signs of Eodan, and didn't seem shocked by her accusations. Gasparo had the same steely look he'd worn when she confronted him at the abattoir. "Just you and Damiano? Funny that you couldn't trust all your friends with the secret. That tells me you know you did something evil."

"Gasparo," Mella began.

Gasparo made a "shut up" gesture with his hand. "Nobody will believe a stranger over their own friends and neighbors," he said. "Go now, and take the werewolf with you, and we won't kill you."

Ginnevra laughed and rolled her shoulders to test the set of her sword. "What, the four of you? That's hilarious."

"We'll see," Gasparo said, drawing a long knife from his belt. Damiano did the same, revealing the shimmer of a silvered blade.

Ginnevra didn't draw her sword. She was faster than they were, and despite her anger over Ciecerella's death and the threat Gasparo had made against Eodan, she didn't want to kill humans if she could help it. "Tell me what you're up to with the dragon," she said. "Why keep it sedated rather than sending for a company to kill it? And why not reveal the secret to the village?"

"I don't understand what's happening," Baldo said. "Gasparo, we can't attack a holy paladin. Put the knife away."

"She's not holy, she's an abomination who sleeps with monsters," Gasparo said. "You know her so-called brother is a were-wolf. She doesn't deserve our respect."

Baldo took a few steps forward. He put his hand on his belt knife, which wasn't long enough to be a threat to anything except maybe a roast chicken. "What did you do to Ciecerella?"

"She would have told everyone what we're doing, Baldo," Damiano said. "Do you want to share the fortune with the whole village? Keep the pittance that would be left once it was divided between everyone? We just wanted her to stay silent for a while—just until the plan was complete. Her death was an accident."

Mella let out a sob and covered her mouth with her hands. "She would never have betrayed us! You never trusted her, that's the truth!"

Gasparo shook his head. "I didn't want her dead," he said, "but that's what had to happen. Mella, don't be a fool. You didn't like her, admit it."

"No, but..." Mella backed up and bumped into one of the bramble piles, making it teeter and the damp thatch slide down its far side. She turned with a gasp, grabbing for it. The others turned to watch, lowering their weapons. Ginnevra plunged forward, seizing Gasparo's wrist and twisting to make the knife fall.

Gasparo threw an awkward, left-handed punch that grazed Ginnevra's temple and blurred her vision for a moment, but she was used to fighting through pain, and the blow barely qualified. She spun Gasparo around, twisting his arm behind his back and forcing him to his knees. Gasparo let out a pained yelp and leaned away from her, reminding her that she'd cracked his rib earlier. "Drop your weapons," she commanded.

Damiano snarled and lunged for her with the silvered knife. He'd had some training, Ginnevra observed with a cold, detached part of her mind, but her instincts had already taken over, and she fended off the blow with her left arm while controlling the wildly struggling Gasparo with her right. Damiano stopped outside her reach, his weapon held in a knife-fighter's grip. Ginnevra kneed Gasparo in the kidney, making him let out a strangled scream as she jogged his broken rib, and drew her pistol. "Give up, Damiano," she said. "Fighting me will make things worse for you."

"You're a damned deviant, and I won't submit to you," Damiano said.

Ginnevra stared him down, her pistol steady, but inside she was worried. She'd never killed a human before, not counting Nucca, and all her instincts screamed against it. But she couldn't let Damiano or the others get away, and she wasn't about to let them kill her. "You two," she said to Baldo and Mella, who hovered near the smoking brambles. "Subdue him, and I won't see you tried for murder."

Baldo and Mella didn't react. Ginnevra didn't dare take her eyes off Damiano, who would come at her the instant she did. She twisted Gasparo's arm harder, making him cry out in pain and thrash harder, which was the opposite of what she'd wanted.

Gasparo suddenly stopped thrashing and sagged. Startled, Ginnevra looked down. Damiano leaped for her. Gasparo twisted and nearly broke free. And a black shape hurtled toward them, plunging toward Damiano.

"No!" Ginnevra shouted. She shoved Gasparo to one side and fired at Damiano. The shot struck him high in the right side of his chest. Damiano gasped and dropped the knife, clutching his chest. In the next moment, Eodan was on him, knocking him prone. Baldo and Mella screamed and ran, stumbling into another smoker and taking it down with them as they fell.

Ginnevra hurried to Eodan's side. "He's not dead," she said. "I think we can save him. I want him to stand trial."

Eodan was growling, a long, low rumbling sound that triggered

Ginnevra's most primal fears. She reminded herself that Eodan wasn't going to attack her and added, "You need to let him up."

Still growling, Eodan backed away. Ginnevra rolled Damiano onto his back. Blood spread across the front of his shirt, and his tanned complexion was chalky. Ginnevra prodded the wound. "It's not—"

Sharp pain shot through her lower back, below where the chain-mail had hiked up as she knelt. Ginnevra gasped and turned to see Gasparo, clutching Damiano's silvered knife, backing away, a look of triumph on his face. The knife was bloody along most of its length. Ginnevra put a hand to her back; it, too, came away bloody. "You fool," she said hoarsely.

Gasparo's look of triumph turned to horror. He backed away a few steps, and then Eodan was on him, snapping at the hand that held the blade. Ginnevra lunged at Gasparo, but her legs weren't working properly and her vision was foggy as if the wind had suddenly changed direction, blowing the smoke toward her. She heard Eodan yelp in pain, a cry that cut her to the heart, and with monumental effort got to her unsteady feet and stumbled to his side.

Blood streaked Eodan's fur from his shoulder all the way down his right foreleg. Gasparo clutched his left wrist, which now ended in a stump. His hand, still holding the knife, lay a couple of feet to one side. Ginnevra put a hand on Eodan's bloody shoulder. He was shaking, and his eyes were closed, but the wound itself didn't look too bad, just gory.

Ginnevra knelt beside Gasparo, whose grip on his maimed wrist slackened as he fell unconscious. She wrestled her chainmail off and yanked at her sleeve, cursing the strength of the seam. With another oath, she snatched the silvered blade from its gruesome location and slashed the fabric, then tore the sleeve off and bound Gasparo's wrist tightly. "Check Damiano," she said curtly, and Eodan left her side, staggering slightly.

Ginnevra's back was a long streak of pain she ignored. She would need to bind the wound soon or risk fainting from blood loss, but paladins were tougher than the average person, and even if Gasparo's attack had perforated a kidney, which she guessed it had, she could endure long enough to see her captives secured.

"He'll need the ball removed," Eodan said from behind her. Ginnevra checked to make sure Gasparo's stump wasn't bleeding heavily anymore, then turned. Eodan knelt beside Damiano, his fingers pressed to the side of the man's throat to check his pulse. Eodan's shoulder and side were covered in blood, and he moved stiffly. "But you're right, he may survive this."

Ginnevra surveyed the clearing. Mella and Baldo were gone, but they'd left signs of their passing in several of the smoking heaps being overturned. "I'm just as glad not to have to deal with them for now," she said, mostly to herself.

She got to her feet and stumbled to where Damiano lay. Eodan put out a hand to stop her falling. "That's a bad wound."

"It's a scratch. It's nothing," Ginnevra lied. "I should cut the ball out. You certainly can't."

Eodan twitched, and she looked his way in time to see his jaw tighten as if she'd struck him. She reviewed what she'd said, and her heart sank. "That's not what I meant," she said. "You're not—"

"We need to get your wound bandaged before you fall over," Eodan said, his voice hard and emotionless. "Give me your other sleeve."

Ginnevra realized she was still holding the knife. She cut away her sleeve and handed it to Eodan. Eodan folded it into a pad and pressed it to Ginnevra's lower back. "Your belt," he said. Ginnevra unfastened her belt, sliding the pistol case free and dropping it on the ground, and refastened it over the pad, tightening it until it hurt. Her vision was still a little foggy, but this time she knew it was because of the smokers, because she also felt slightly drowsy.

Eodan rose and strode to Gasparo's side. The man had begun to stir, but Eodan ignored his feeble movements, instead taking his maimed arm and examining the stump. "I was careless, and he hit me once before I took off his hand," he said.

"Yes, and speaking of wounds, yours is still bleeding," Ginnevra said. She didn't want to point out that the silver in it would exacerbate the injury. She'd already called him a monster too many times that day.

Eodan nodded. He turned to face Ginnevra, and his eyes widened. "Ginnevra," he said, "come here. Don't move quickly, but you need to get over here *now*."

He was looking past her, past the smokers. Cold dread filled Ginnevra, and despite his words, she turned. A wide gap in the line of smokers where Mella and Baldo had overturned two of them was completely free of gray smoke. Trails of green gas filled the gap, and poking its head through the empty space was the dragon.

SIXTEEN

G innevra slowly knelt up from her position beside Damiano. The dragon's yellow eyes glowed like lamps, its gaze piercing the green gas wreathing its head. Its head bobbed like a cork in water, swaying to and fro on its serpentine neck. Ginnevra got to her feet, moving as slowly as she could without falling over. The stink of the green gas, too-sweet, wafted over her, sickening her. She took a step backward, then another, and reached for her sword.

"Don't," Eodan said, his voice forceful but not very loud. The dragon's attention immediately focused on him. Ginnevra took advantage of its distraction to draw her sword. With her other hand, she reached for the semiconscious Damiano's ankle. She wasn't going to leave him as a helpless target.

Damiano moved then, reaching for Ginnevra. "Help," he croaked.

The dragon turned on them, tilting its head like an inquisitive bird. Ginnevra wanted to point out she *was* helping the man, but the dragon's hearing was clearly acute. "Shut up," she whispered.

Damiano arched his neck to look behind him. His body stiffened when he saw the dragon, and he screamed. The dragon jerked and took a step back as if the noise had startled it. Then it came toward them, staggering like a drunkard but intent on Damiano.

Ginnevra grabbed Damiano around the waist and hauled him over her shoulder. The dragon's hot, stinking breath engulfed her, and the sickness redoubled. Damiano, still screaming, inhaled a lungful of green gas and convulsed, over and over again. Ginnevra, staggering under Damiano's not inconsiderable weight as well as her own weakened condition, took a few steps backward, tripped, and dropped her burden and her sword.

She heard Eodan running toward her and shouted, "Stay back! The gas will kill you if you're in human shape!" Again, she reached for Damiano's ankles and cried out when his booted foot, still thrashing, caught her on the chin, knocking her on her rear end.

The dragon's glowing eyes focused on Damiano, whose convulsions were weakening. Ginnevra's hand fell on her sword hilt. She snatched it up and leaped in front of Damiano's body. "Back off," she said, though she was sure the dragon didn't understand her words. She was just as sure it understood nearly four feet of silvered steel.

The dragon stopped. Green gas trickled from its nostrils, but it didn't open its mouth to breathe out more. Yellow eyes regarded Ginnevra steadily. Ginnevra didn't budge. Behind her, Damiano stopped moving. She hoped he wasn't dead, but she knew deep down that was a futile hope. She couldn't hear Eodan anymore. With luck, that meant he'd changed shape to something not as vulnerable.

The dragon's head drew back. It let out another of those strange, croaking cries, then sagged to the ground, its one wing furling around its back, the other drooping. Unlike before, it didn't fall into unconsciousness. It kept watching Ginnevra, blinking slowly, occasional tremors flicking through its good wing.

Ginnevra stood, not letting down her guard, until the constant breeze through the clearing blew most of the gas back toward the dragon. Then she knelt with her eyes never leaving the dragon's, stripped one glove off, and felt along Damiano's wrist for a pulse. She didn't find one. She couldn't hear his heart beat. Carefully, she felt her way up his chest, past the bloody wound to his face. No air sighed in and out of his mouth. Ginnevra tried to summon up grief for the death of a human and came up empty.

She stood again. The dragon hadn't moved. Ginnevra watched it closely, saw how its chest heaved as if breathing was difficult, how the glow of its eyes was dimmed now because its nictitating membranes had slid shut. She saw how still it held its injured wing. Then she lowered her sword and walked forward.

Behind her, Eodan let out a sound midway between a howl and a yelp that she guessed was meant as either warning or protest. She ignored him and kept walking. In the next moment, he was in front of her, barring her way, his teeth bared in a snarl.

Ginnevra stopped. "It's helpless," she said, "and I don't think it would attack even if it was capable. Whatever else it is, it's not a monster. And neither are you. I'm sorry I made you believe I felt otherwise." She stepped wide around him and kept walking. Eodan didn't try to stop her again.

When she was about ten feet from the dragon, she slowly set her blade on the ground, not wanting to frighten the creature any more than she already had, and tugged her other glove off and tossed it aside. With both hands spread wide in a gesture she hoped was non-threatening, she walked the final few paces and rested one hand on the dragon's shoulder.

Once again, it shuddered and let out that croaking sound. "It's all right," Ginnevra said, and then felt foolish, because it couldn't understand her. "I want to help."

Footsteps sounded behind her, and Eodan said, "What exactly do you intend to do?"

"I don't know. But I can't leave it like this." Ginnevra ran her hand along the dragon's hide. It was rough and felt like cracked, dry skin, hotter even than Eodan, without the slightest give. She wished she knew if this was normal for dragons.

Eodan put a hand on Ginnevra's shoulder. "There may not be anything we *can* do. I think it's dying."

Ginnevra clenched her jaw against unexpected tears. "Those fools," she said, her voice thick. "Where's Gasparo?"

"Ginnevra," Eodan said, but Ginnevra had already whirled and was striding across the clearing to Gasparo. He was conscious again, and had managed to sit up, cradling his maimed arm across his chest.

"You bitch," he said when she approached. "I'll see you—"

Ginnevra slapped him so hard his head snapped back. "Why did you do it?" she demanded. "You wanted its treasure? Or was it for the fun of killing a legendary monster?"

"Treasure?" Gasparo sounded incredulous. "Do you have any idea what rich fools will pay for ground dragon bone? Or dragon's blood?"

Ginnevra felt sicker than before. "You were going to...to harvest it?"

"Hard to kill a dragon," Gasparo said. "But it took longer than we thought to die of starvation. It's not a crime, killing a monster. Not like what you've done, setting a vicious werewolf on a human when you're sworn to protect us. I'll make sure everyone knows what you are."

Fury and disgust surged through Ginnevra, and she found her hand had strayed to her hip where the pistol used to be. That sobered her instantly. No matter how evil and horrible humans were, a paladin was sworn to protect them, not execute vigilante justice. She closed her eyes and prayed silently for calm. Then she turned her back on Gasparo without saying anything and returned to the dragon's side.

Eodan had moved to where its wing hung uselessly beside it. "It let me touch it," he said, sounding amazed. "The bone hasn't healed right."

"Can you do anything about that?"

Eodan shook his head. "Based on my examination, such as it was, it's been at least seven weeks since the bone broke. The only way to fix it is to re-break it and set it properly. And I have no idea how to do either of those things, not to mention the kind of distress we'd inflict on it."

"And it's starving to death," Ginnevra said. "We should feed it."

"Feed it what? It's too weak to hunt and probably too weak to tear its prey apart. It's not a baby bird fallen out of the nest. It's a dragon."

Ginnevra walked forward until she was near its head. The green gas didn't smell quite as awful now. "Then what are we supposed to do?"

Eodan didn't follow her. "Put it out of its misery," he said.

Ginnevra spun to stare at him, for once not caring that he was naked. "Kill it?"

Eodan took a step forward, then another, and stopped. "It's starving, it's in pain, and it can't fly. There's no way we can fix that. We probably couldn't have saved it even if we'd been the ones to find it right after its wing broke instead of Gasparo and his cronies."

"But…" Ginnevra looked over her shoulder at the dragon, who was watching her as intently as if it could understand their words. It wouldn't be that calm if it could. "None of this is right. It's not a monster. It doesn't deserve this fate."

Eodan shook his head. "No. But this is how it ends sometimes. You're a paladin, Ginnevra. You face the hard truths so others don't have to."

His words sent a chill through her. She was a paladin. She had a duty. But this couldn't possibly be what the Goddess meant when She sent Her warriors into the world to protect humanity. And yet, what else could Ginnevra do?

She remembered shooting Nucca, and the memory burned within her. That, too, had been a mercy killing, saving Nucca's spirit at the cost of killing her body. Eodan was right—sometimes that was how things ended.

She picked up her sword. It felt as if it weighed five times what it did, the tip pulling down so it dragged through the matted bracken where the dragon had lain for so many weeks. She faced the dragon and made herself look at it dispassionately, searching for weaknesses the way she would any monster.

It was pointless to attack its hide, she decided, remembering how that hide had felt under her hand. It was too tough, and while she might be able to force the sword through one of those cracks, she couldn't count on reaching a vital organ that way. Blunt force might work, but she'd left her mace in the cottage and she didn't think she could keep her resolve if she had to go all the way back for it. The dragon wouldn't sit still for suffocation, even if she could manage that.

But those big, yellow eyes, and the brain that lay behind them—that, she could do.

Ginnevra walked forward until she stood next to its head. The dragon regarded her through those milky white membranes. They gave it the look of a monster, the way so many of the Bright One's creations had those white eyes that marked them as Hers. It made this a little easier.

"I'm sorry," she whispered, and raised her sword for a killing thrust.

The dragon let out another croaking cry and moved its head, almost as if it welcomed what Ginnevra intended to do to it. Ginnevra blinked away tears that made the dragon suddenly wavery. She drew back her blade. This was how it had to end.

And in that moment, she made a different choice.

She threw her sword aside. "Goddess!" she shouted, throwing her head back to address the dark, starlit sky. "I ask a boon!"

Nothing happened. Ginnevra drew in a deep breath that was still slightly scented with gas. Maybe this was pointless. The moon had set hours ago, leaving the sky empty. She had no reason to expect a response, let alone one granting her request. But if she didn't ask, she'd never know.

"You granted me Your power to defend the innocent," she continued. "I thought that meant killing monsters, and I didn't understand why my grace shattered when I did exactly what I was sworn to do. I think I know the meaning now. Losing my grace wasn't a punishment—it was an opportunity to choose a new path. To learn that the world is greater than I believed. Thank You."

Even the insects had gone silent. Ginnevra heard nothing but her own breathing and the rasping, gravelly breathing of the dragon. "I don't understand theology," she said. "The battle between You and Your bright sister—that's beyond me. But I do know that the struggle isn't as simple as the fight between humans and monsters. Some of the Bright One's creations choose to turn against her." She thought of Gasparo and Damiano and their plan to kill a dragon. "And some of Your people are more evil than I'm sure You'd like."

She licked her dry lips, swallowed to moisten her throat, and said, "You are our example of justice and compassion, Dark Lady. I beg of You, show compassion to this creature. Heal its wounds so it can fly free."

She waited. The wind gusted through the clearing again, driving away the smoke and the green gas. Behind her, Eodan moved, and she hoped he would have the good sense to stay still.

The wind blew harder, buffeting her. In its voice, she heard, *Why?*

She didn't question whether it was her imagination. "There is no why," she responded. "Sometimes it's the way things end."

Again, the wind spoke: *what will you give?*

Ginnevra swallowed again. "What You choose to take," she said. "I owe You everything, and I'll sacrifice it if that's what You require." She wondered if she'd just made a huge mistake. Give up her paladin's gifts, maybe her life, for the sake of a creature who wouldn't understand her sacrifice?

The wind nearly lifted her off her feet, making her close her eyes against its power. *Enough*, the wind said, and vanished, shaking Ginnevra where she'd been braced against it. She opened her eyes on darkness. At first, she thought the wind had blown out the torches. Then she realized she saw nothing, not even the dragon right in front of her. Terror shot through her, followed by grief. She'd lost her paladin's endowments. She hoped the sacrifice was worth it.

She took a step forward, her hands in front of her and her eyes wide open in the hope that she'd eventually acclimate to the darkness, and ran into the dragon's side. It was warmer than she remembered and felt more flexible. She couldn't smell the gas anymore, which was a small blessing, though not one she was enthusiastic about. Though if she wasn't a paladin anymore, she wasn't immune to the gas, so maybe she should be grateful for the small things.

Then the darkness deepened. Ginnevra didn't know how that was possible, because dark was dark, but somehow there was depth to the midnight blackness that surrounded her, as if she had stepped from an unlit, windowless small room into a fathomless cavern deep underground. Fear gave way to curiosity, a desire to understand this odd experience. She raised her chin and strained to see something, anything that would give dimension to the blackness.

The darkness shifted, an impossible feeling, but that was the only way to describe how it felt to be wrapped in something velvety soft that embraced her with a warmth that reminded her of home and family and love. She closed her eyes against tears of happiness that overpowered her misery.

When she opened her eyes, the darkness was gone, and she could see clearly despite the torches having gone out. The dragon lay before her, perfectly still. Ginnevra's joy at not having lost her gifts faded as she realized her prayer hadn't been answered. She tried to tell herself it had always been unlikely that the Goddess would care about a monster, even if it wasn't really a monster, but her heart felt leaden and her eyes ached with more tears.

The dragon opened its eyes. Then it rose to its feet, steadily and without a single quiver.

Ginnevra gasped and took a step back, bumping into Eodan, who gripped her shoulders to keep her from falling over. The dragon extended its serpentine neck to its full length, tilting its head skyward. With a tremendous rush of air, both wings lifted and snapped open, the green membranes gleaming with light that came from nowhere Ginnevra could see.

The dragon's head snaked down to face Ginnevra. The green gas no longer trickled from its mouth and nostrils. The yellow glow of its eyes was brighter now, no longer dimmed by either membranes or starvation. It stared Ginnevra full in the face, blinking once. Then it ducked its head and butted against her chest, for all the world like a cat looking to be petted.

Astonished, Ginnevra laid her hand on its broad nose. The hide no longer felt dry and cracked. They stood like that for a moment, dragon and human, until the dragon backed away and leaped into the sky, its great wings beating for altitude. Ginnevra watched it fly away until even she could no longer see it silhouetted against the star-filled brilliance of the moonless sky.

She'd forgotten Eodan was there until he let go of her shoulders. When she turned around, he was in wolf shape again. She couldn't think of anything to say that wouldn't sound stupid or anticlimactic. Finally, she said, "I'll take Gasparo back to the village to confine him. Will you see if you can find those other two? It sounds like they weren't in on the murder, but I think they deserve some kind of punishment for what they did to the dragon."

Eodan nodded and ran off northward.

Ginnevra crossed the clearing to where Gasparo lay, clutching his maimed arm. "What did you do?" he whispered. "That monster—"

"It wasn't a monster, and you should feel guilty over torturing it," she said. "But what's going to happen is you'll be tried for Ciecerella's murder. And say whatever you like about Eodan. No one will believe you over me."

He gestured with the stump. "That thing bit my hand off!"

"Dragon bite," Ginnevra said. "Or I cut it off because you attacked me. Trust me, Gasparo, you've lost. And I hope you receive justice. It just won't be from me." She hauled him to his feet and nearly lost her own balance. Her various pains were starting to catch up with her, not to mention the blood loss. But she felt more at peace than she had in a long time.

CHAPTER

SEVENTEEN

aghinardo's sleepiness, when Ginnevra pounded on his door at nearly midnight, vanished when he saw Gasparo's condition and heard Ginnevra's abbreviated version of the story. She enjoyed his astonishment almost as much as she enjoyed his prompt response to her request for guards and a cottage with a door that locked. Gasparo didn't say anything about werewolves, and of his hand Ginnevra said only that there'd been a fight. Maghinardo's shocked expression clearly said he thought Gasparo was mad to have fought a paladin, but he didn't ask any more questions.

Mella and Bardo walked into the village as Ginnevra was supervising Gasparo's confinement. They both looked to be in shock, but they walked straight to Ginnevra and swore they'd had no part in Ciecerella's murder. "We just wanted to make a little money," Bardo said. "It's not wrong, turning a monster's death to a human advantage, is it?"

He sounded so afraid—afraid of what she might do to him—and gripped Mella's hand so tightly Ginnevra's anger drained away. "Go back and retrieve Damiano's body," she told them. "Clear away those foul smokers. And hope the Goddess has mercy on you, because if it were up to me, I surely would not."

They both bowed inappropriately low and scurried away. Ginnevra hoped the Goddess would find that punishment, such as it was, sufficient. She'd had her fill of death for one night.

With Gasparo securely locked away and Mella and Bardo dealt with, Ginnevra could explain to Maghinardo in more detail. On the long walk back to Arrus from the clearing, she'd thought about what to say. Her prayer to the Goddess, and the Goddess's response, felt personal and private as well as being difficult to explain. But the more she thought about it, the more convinced she became that while treasuring secrets was dear to the Goddess's heart, there were some secrets that ought not to be kept.

So she told Maghinardo about Gasparo and Damiano's plan to kill the dragon, about how that had affected the monsters plaguing Arrus, and what had happened when Ginnevra arrived. She told him about Ciecerella's death and how Damiano and Gasparo had intended to kill Ginnevra as well. And she told him how the Goddess had intervened to save the life of something everyone believed to be a monster.

"I'm not saying you need to give the benefit of the doubt to something that's trying to kill you," she said. "But remember that the Goddess gives Her gifts where She chooses, and don't be afraid to ask Her blessing for yourselves."

Maghinardo nodded, his eyes wide with astonishment. "But how could you know the dragon wouldn't kill you when it was healed?" he asked. "My lady, surely even for you that's dangerous."

"I had faith," Ginnevra said. She realized that was a non-answer, but the real answer *was* personal and private and none of his business.

She trudged back through the village and around the fields. She hadn't found the pistol case, but she had retrieved the pistol and now held it in one hand while the other steadied the sword so it wouldn't bang against the wound in her back. Her chainmail lay draped over her arm, weighing her pistol hand down, but putting it back on felt impossible, especially given her wound.

Weariness, the aftereffects of fighting and grieving and addressing her Goddess, overtook her about halfway to her cottage, and she stopped between two fields and stood for a few minutes, considering the benefits of simply lying down where she was and sleeping until morning. But she realized through the haze of pain and exhaustion that she'd sleep more comfortably, and heal more quickly, if she was in her own bed. She made herself put one foot in front of the other until she was at her cottage door.

Eodan was seated on the hearth, fully dressed. He stood when she entered, but made no move toward her. Feeling dull and mentally numb, Ginnevra nodded at him. The events of the afternoon seemed a year in the past. "Are you responsible for Mella and Bardo returning to the village?"

"I herded them in that direction and hoped they'd take it as a sign," Eodan said. "I'm not sure what it would be a sign of, but it sounds like it worked."

Ginnevra nodded again. She let the chainmail slide off her arm to puddle on the floor in a jingling heap, then set the pistol on the table and unbuckled the sword belt. Eodan took the sword from her as it slipped through her fingers, careful to touch only the hilt and the sheath. He turned to prop it in the corner. Spots of blood showed on his shirt, and without thinking, Ginnevra said, "Did you need help bandaging your wound?"

Eodan didn't turn around. He said, "I managed it. Let me look at your back."

Ginnevra stood firm. "You're still bleeding. Let me help you first. Then you'll be more efficient at treating me."

Eodan shook his head, but in a way that suggested he didn't have an argument. He pulled off his shirt, revealing an awkwardly-wrapped bandage around his shoulder.

Ginnevra pushed him to sit on a stool and removed the bandage.

The knife wound was shallow but long, and streaks of dried blood showed where Eodan hadn't been able to reach it to clean it properly. Ginnevra fetched a clean cloth, poured water into a bowl, and deftly cleaned and bandaged his shoulder.

Despite her weariness, she felt a heightened awareness of his closeness, of how smooth and warm his skin was beneath her fingers and how the werewolf musk was stronger after his exertions. She made herself look at him as dispassionately as she had the dragon. It didn't work. She still could think of nothing but how it had felt to kiss him and how much she wanted to do it again.

She tied off the bandage and rinsed the cloth in pink water. Eodan took the cloth from her. "Sit," he said.

Ginnevra sat and pulled her shirt up to give him access to the wound. She thought about taking her shirt off entirely—that would be more convenient, yes? But she knew it wouldn't be about convenience, and he still seemed angry with her. So she gathered her shirt below her breasts and stopped herself wincing when he removed the makeshift dressing and prodded at the injury.

Now that she was sitting, exhaustion caught up with her. Only the pain of being poked where the knife had gone in kept her from falling asleep. Along with the exhaustion came a terrible, heart-rending ache in her chest. She should have told him how she felt earlier, and never mind if he was ready to talk. Now it was clearly too late. He'd no doubt be gone when she woke in the morning, and she would never see him again. And it wouldn't matter that she'd fallen in love with someone people would think was a monster.

"This penetrated deep," Eodan said. He put a clean pad of folded cloth over the wound and bound it snugly to her body. "I think it reached your kidney. Is that a problem for you?"

"I'll piss red for a few days, but it will heal as well as anything," Ginnevra said. She lowered her shirt and stood, turning to face him. Eodan was washing his hands and didn't look at her. "Thank you," she added. "I'm glad you were there."

Eodan shrugged. "You have the worst sense of self-preservation

I've ever seen," he said without looking up. "Turning your back on an armed enemy. You're lucky he didn't have better aim, or we wouldn't be having this conversation."

It felt like being stabbed again. She was too tired to withstand the unexpected attack. She turned away from him so he wouldn't see her tears and said, "I'm going to bed. Don't wake me when you leave in the morning, all right?"

"When I leave?" Eodan said.

He sounded surprised, and that made the tears fall more heavily. Ginnevra swallowed against her throat closing up. When she felt she could speak clearly, she said, "I don't think there's any more point to you staying, do you? Arrus is safe, and I'll be returning to Abraciabene soon. I hope you have a good life."

He took a step toward her. "Ginnevra—"

"Don't say anything else," Ginnevra said. "Please. I'm sorry I hurt you. I couldn't see beyond what my sister paladins would say if they knew I'd fallen in love with you. But if I don't believe you're a monster, I have to back those words with my actions. I'm sorry I didn't realize that in time."

She put her hand on the door latch. Eodan's quick steps behind her were all the warning she had before he put his hand on her shoulder and turned her around. He drew her into his arms and held her tightly. "I thought he'd killed you," he murmured. "He wouldn't have wounded you if I'd been watching him. You were dead, and it was my fault, and all I could think was how I'd let you die without ever telling you I love you."

She felt numb again, this time with astonishment. "I don't understand," she said, her tired mind foggy and uncomprehending. "You love me—Eodan, why would you love me?"

"Should I make a list?" Eodan chuckled. "I've never known anyone like you. Every time I think I have you figured out, you surprise me. Your courage, your strength, your compassion—everything about you brings me joy, and I love you more with every passing day."

"But—I mean, you shouldn't feel that way—I turned my back on you and treated you like a monster—"

"That hurt. A lot." His arms tightened around her. "Then I let myself consider what it must be like for you, kissing someone everyone you know would shun you for loving, or worse. But by then, we were about to face those murderers, and that's no time to declare love to anyone."

"I thought you hated me. I felt so awful, remembering what I'd done. I really am sorry for hurting you." Ginnevra put her arms around Eodan and rested her head on his unwounded shoulder. "I was so afraid for you, facing Gasparo and that knife."

"I was angry, and that made me careless. But it's not a bad wound, just one that won't heal quickly." Eodan's hand moved to caress her short hair. "And this feels good enough that I barely feel the pain."

She laughed. It did feel wonderful, being held by him, breathing in the scent of him and feeling his powerful body pressed close against hers. "I needed this," she agreed.

"Any time, beloved," he said.

Ginnevra shivered at the endearment. She closed her eyes and let go the last of her sorrow and pain.

She didn't know how long they stood there, holding each other, before she jerked out of a nearly-asleep state. "I have to go to bed," she said, stepping back. Then, feeling shy, she said, "Come with me."

Eodan's eyebrows rose. "I don't think I can manage that," he said, "and you're in no condition for it, either."

Ginnevra smiled and took his hand, marveling once more at how warm it was and how the rough skin of his palm comforted her. "Just to sleep. You're wounded, and you shouldn't sleep on the floor."

"That's tempting even before I consider who I'd share the bed with," Eodan said with a smile. He closed his hand on hers more tightly. "All right. But nothing but sleep. Physician's orders."

"I'm a paladin. We have phenomenal self-control," Ginnevra said with an answering smile.

She woke in the morning feeling warm and relaxed as she hadn't for days. It took her a moment to realize she wasn't alone in her bed. Eodan slept beside her, his arm across her stomach weighing her down. The sight was so unexpectedly erotic she drew in a quick breath she let out slowly, not wanting to wake him. He looked so good, his dark hair tangled across his forehead, his short beard framing firm, beautifully shaped lips, his cheekbones well defined and his nose straight as hers was not. She didn't think it was love that made him seem the handsomest man she'd ever seen.

She watched him for a while, drinking him in, until he blinked, shifted his position, and tightened his arm across her. His gaze fell on her, and he smiled, a lazy, provocative smile that sent a rush of pleasure through her. "I don't know which is better, the bed or the company," he said.

"It's definitely the company," Ginnevra said. "I've been sleeping alone in this bed for several weeks, and this is the most rested I've ever felt."

"Sleeping alone," Eodan repeated, and put his arm around her shoulders. "That's almost a crime." Gently, he pulled her close for a kiss.

She settled in to lie next to him, kissing him and running her fingers along the line of his jaw, enjoying the sensation of his beard against her skin. Eodan's hands trailed down her spine to her hips and then took hold of the hem of her shirt, slipping beneath it. His fingers were warm enough to feel like he was drawing trails of fire across her skin. "I though the physician said no sex," she murmured, though she didn't stop him touching her.

"There are any number of things we can do that stop short of intercourse," Eodan said, his fingers gradually moving northward. "And I've dreamed of doing this since the night we fought the maligna. The first time you touched me."

Ginnevra gasped as his hands brushed more sensitive skin. "Well, in that case," she said, and Eodan stopped her words with another kiss.

EVENTUALLY, THEY ROSE AND ATE BREAKFAST, SITTING ACROSS FROM EACH other at the table. Ginnevra couldn't remember the last time she'd felt so happy. Her lips curved in a smile every time she looked at him, a smile that grew wider when his eyes met hers. How odd that she'd ever found his blue eyes strange.

"So, what happens next?" Eodan asked when the meal was over and he was tidying away plates.

"I'll have to take Gasparo in for trial. There's a town half a day's journey on foot from here called Sarenzo where I can get horses, and then Negozente has a justiciary where they can deal with him." Ginnevra stretched gingerly, careful not to strain her wound. "And after that, I have to go to Abraciabene. To report."

Eodan stilled. "What will you tell them?"

Ginnevra bit her lip in thought. "The truth, of course. About what happened here, about the dragon. About the two of us. Unless..."

"Unless?" Eodan raised his eyebrows, inviting her to continue.

Ginnevra drew a deep breath. "Unless this is all there is between us. Eodan, I don't know how we can make a life together. I don't even know if that's what you want. Maybe it's better we separate now, before life breaks both our hearts."

Eodan regarded her steadily. Then he sat on the hearth and gestured for her to sit beside him. "I think I need to make something clear," he said. "Werewolves don't make romantic connections lightly. We mate for life and we are perfectly faithful within that bond. Until this week, I'd never found anyone I wanted to share my life with, and now the thought of leaving you fills me with horror. I love you, Ginnevra, and I will never desert you."

Ginnevra realized she was holding her breath and released it. Eodan took her hands in his, his blue-eyed gaze intent on her. "I know that's not what you expected," he said, "and if it's not what you want, it's not binding on you. If we need to go separate ways, if that's your choice, I'll abide by it. But you should know I'm willing to endure whatever it takes to stay by your side."

"I—" Ginnevra's heart pounded so hard she was sure he could hear it. "You're serious."

Eodan nodded.

She shifted her hands so she could clasp his in return. "I don't know what's waiting for me in Abraciabene," she said. "If I'm still a paladin, I have duties. I don't know how we'll manage to stay together, if I'm off on missions and you're...I can barely imagine you living in some human city."

"I do have marketable skills," Eodan said. "Physicians are welcome anywhere."

Ginnevra couldn't help smiling at his wry expression. "But what about the full moon? And you'd be leaving your pack behind for good. I know they cast you out, but you still feel some connection."

"There's nothing more I can do for the other outcasts, and nothing could persuade me to sacrifice myself to worship the Bright Goddess," Eodan said. "As for the time of the full moon, I don't know. But we can figure it out. Together."

His utter certainty and the look in his eyes shook her to her core. "I don't want you to go," she said. "I love you. And I'll go on loving you no matter what the Blessed says."

Eodan's smile disappeared. "She won't cast you out," he said. "Not after what I saw last night."

"She might," Ginnevra said, trying to sound casual at the possibility of losing almost everything that made her who she was. "I have to have faith that whatever happens, it's in service to the Dark Lady."

She'd never wanted more to say that her future was in the Goddess's hands, but that would be counter to everything she believed in. There was no destiny. There was only the moment, and it was what you made it.

CHAPTER

EIGHTEEN

F our days later, they rode into Abraciabene in the middle of a torrential summer rainstorm that caught them off guard and far from shelter. Almost no one shared the road with them, and the rains had driven the beggars indoors. The guards at the gate beckoned them through without more than a glance; they huddled within the little guard houses flanking the gate and barely poked their noses out into the storm.

Ginnevra watched Eodan guide his horse through the streets of the outer city without any sign that he'd never ridden a horse until three days ago. They'd had a difficult few minutes when buying the animals when it turned out horses knew predators when they smelled them. After disrupting a couple of stables in Negozente, sending their horses into near-panic, they'd finally found this placid gelding who was almost as unruffled as a paladin's mount and, even better, was big enough to carry Eodan easily. Ginnevra, who'd started to have visions of Eodan walking to Abraciabene, felt relieved enough not to care about how expensive the horse was.

They chose the first inn they came to, a sizable building with a large stable yard whose packed earth was rapidly becoming soup. A lanky stable hand ran out from the covered stalls to urge them under cover. "You both look near drowned," he said with a grin that displayed a gap between his front teeth. "Here, dry off some before you go inside. Innkeeper gets frosty when people drip on his floors. He's got pretensions to inner city manners."

Ginnevra thanked him for the blanket he handed her. She and Eodan stood in an empty stall and rubbed away rainwater fiercely. Eodan's new clothes, bought in Negozente, fit him better than the ones he'd stolen, and Ginnevra stole an admiring look at how his wet shirt clung to his broad shoulders.

Less admiring and more concerned, she eyed the sodden bandage covering the knife wound that showed no sign of healing yet. Her own injury still bothered her, but it had been deep enough she hadn't expected to be free of it for another week. She couldn't help comparing Eodan's wound to the injuries the maligna had inflicted on him, how those had disappeared after only a few days. Eodan didn't seem disturbed about his wound, and she figured he would know better than she what to expect from the influence of the silver poison, but she still worried.

Eodan pushed his damp hair out of his face and said, "I'll take a room here. You don't need me along for this."

"That's not true. I need you very much. But they'll all know—" She glanced at the stable hand, busily caring for their horses and not apparently listening. "They'll all know what you are," she said in a lower voice, "and they won't wait on an explanation before attacking you."

"That's what I meant." Eodan draped the soaked blanket over the stall door. "Will you go immediately?"

"As soon as the rain lets up, yes. I don't think I could bear to wait." She blew out her breath, raking her fingers through her short hair to tame it. "I may have to wait regardless. The Blessed is very busy."

"It will all work out," Eodan said. He put his arms around Ginnevra and drew her close.

"We don't think that way," Ginnevra said. "It's like expecting a certain future."

"I know. But that's not what I mean." Eodan kissed her lightly. "I mean that at some point, this moment will be in the past, and you'll have reached the moment that to us is in the future. And there's nothing we can do to stop that happening, so there's no point worrying about it."

Ginnevra smiled. "You're halfway to being a paladin yourself, reasoning like that."

"You're such a bad influence," Eodan said, straight-faced.

Arms around each other, they watched the rain fall until the torrent faded to a sprinkle and then vanished. The clouds still obscured the sky, but watery sunlight filled the air, and the fresh smell of earth after rain, washing away the stink even the holy city couldn't escape, filled Ginnevra with confidence.

The innkeeper didn't do more than look warily at them when they entered, carrying their gear. Ginnevra judged it was their still-wet appearance and not Eodan's race that did it. She had had to remind herself multiple times over the last few days that no one who wasn't a paladin or an anointed could possibly guess Eodan was a werewolf just by looking, and the werewolf musk was strong only to her enhanced senses. Still, every time they had to interact with an innkeeper or tavern owner, she tensed, waiting for a conflict.

Her nervous worry didn't seem to bother Eodan at all. He was always friendly and direct with the people they met, making pleasant conversation and behaving like a human. On the second night, after seeing Gasparo turned over to the justiciary, Ginnevra had asked Eodan whether he'd had much practice pretending to be human, given how good he was at it.

"None," Eodan had said, and to her astonished reaction, he had added, "One thing I know is that people, werewolf or human, like to talk about themselves. So I ask questions and act interested, and everyone is always too busy telling me about their lives to wonder at my occasional missteps."

"That's...really clever," Ginnevra had said. "I never noticed that before."

"Well, that, and humans are remarkably oblivious about even the things that are right in front of them," Eodan had said. "You're all caught up in worries about what others will think."

Ginnevra had pretended to snarl at him, but she had to admit he was right.

Now, watching him negotiate with the innkeeper for a room, she was struck unexpectedly by a flash of love for him. She would never have guessed she might fall in love so easily; she'd always had trouble getting close to men she was interested in, and never let that closeness go anywhere serious. Eodan had taken her by surprise.

He turned at that moment, and his eyes lit up. She realized she was smiling a fond, silly smile and blushed, but didn't turn away. Eodan took her hand and led her down a dark hall to a door with no lock. It was small, with two beds crammed into a space better suited to one, but it smelled clean and the bedding, when Ginnevra prodded at it, was free of vermin.

She changed into a dry shirt and then set the sack containing her armor on one of the beds and began removing it, piece by piece, laying it out across the bed to examine it. It didn't look any more battered than usual; she kept it in good condition as all paladins did, honoring the Goddess's symbolic gift of strength by not letting it fall into disrepair.

Eodan sat on the bed opposite, watching her dry and polish the plate. "I've never seen you wear it," he said.

"I was never in the right position to use it," Ginnevra said absently. "Fortunately, it's made to be donned without assistance." She put on the dark red gambeson and slipped into the chainmail sleeves that fastened across her chest and back, then buckled the cuirass into place.

"It's beautiful," Eodan said. "Though, granted, I say that the way I'd say it about that dragon—beautiful and deadly."

Ginnevra grinned. "Yes, no hugs now." She swiftly donned spaulders, cuisses, greaves, and vambraces, tugging each piece to make it lie properly. After a moment's thought, she left off the coif and helmet. She wanted to show respect for the Goddess, but she also wanted to show humility, and going bareheaded accomplished that.

Properly outfitted, she strapped her sword over her shoulder and shrugged one last time to test the fit. The pistol, she left in its new case on the bed. If she ended up in a position where she needed it, she'd likely be dead and the pistol would be irrelevant.

Eodan stood as she tugged on her gloves. "Good luck," he said. "I'll be waiting."

She was afraid if she said anything, it would come out shaky, not because she was afraid but because her nerves hadn't gotten the message about not worrying for the future. She also wished she dared kiss him, but being cased in silvered steel put an end to that wish. So she smiled and waited for him to step aside before exiting.

The innkeeper's eyes widened and his mouth hung slack when he saw her walk through the tiny entrance hall. "My lady," he managed, "I didn't..."

Ginnevra guessed he hadn't given them the best room in the house because he'd taken them for little better than vagrants. "It's all right," she said. "Please have food sent to my companion, and I'll be back..." She didn't know how to end that sentence. She nodded politely and left the inn.

Trade had resumed once the storm had passed, and the narrow, winding streets were as full as ever of men and women buying, selling, trading, shouting at one another, and bickering over prices. They didn't fall silent when she passed, but they did get out of her way at speed. It would have amused Ginnevra if she hadn't been sick with dread. She commanded her stomach to stop being stupid and strode as rapidly as she could toward the inner gate.

This time, the men and women waiting to pass through to the inner city made way for her in silence. Ginnevra took advantage of their courtesy, judging it equal courtesy to accept the honor they did her. Goddess alone knew whether she was still worthy of it, but in a sense, they were doing honor to the Goddess, not to her, and that was not something she felt comfortable rejecting.

She saluted the guards at the gate, who returned her salute in stunned silence. She'd been half afraid they'd challenge her, because she didn't know what to say about the business that brought her there. But they simply stood aside and let her pass.

The peace of the inner city calmed her nerves somewhat, though that was offset by how many people stared at her and whispered things her enhanced hearing heard clearly: "...paladin alone..." and "...wonder what she's doing here..." and "...suppose she's under condemnation, I've never seen a paladin walk when she could ride." Ginnevra had left her horse at the inn, not sure she should take advantage of the paladins' hostelry for a horse not belonging to the sisterhood. Now she wondered if she'd made the wrong choice. Too late to do anything about it now.

She was the only one at the Bastion gate that afternoon, but the guards in their blue and black surcoats stopped her anyway. "Your business, my lady?"

Here it came. "I'm here to speak with the Blessed on a private matter."

"Is the Blessed expecting you?" the female guard said.

"No. And yes. It's to do with a mission she assigned me, but the time of my arrival was not planned." Ginnevra's heart beat harder, and she was grateful these were anointed and not paladins, who would hear her swift heartbeat and believe she meant something underhanded.

The guards looked at each other. "We'll have to send a runner," the male guard said. "Please wait." The female guard stepped through the gate to the guard house, and immediately a child darted away out of sight. It was so much like what had happened on her first visit Ginnevra felt a moment's dissociation, like then and now had collided. She shook the feeling away.

Ginnevra stepped to the side and assumed a parade rest position she could hold for hours. She hoped she wouldn't be here for hours.

Her heart rate slowed now that she'd passed the first hurdle. She wished Eodan were there even as she was grateful he hadn't come. The anointed might not have the extraordinary senses of a paladin, but they might still know a werewolf when they saw one. And even if they didn't, Ginnevra still balked at the idea of bringing one into the Blessed's presence. It had nothing to do with whether or not were-wolves were monsters and everything to do with the fact that Eodan's people were the pinnacle of creation by the Dark Lady's enemy. Ginnevra simply could not do it.

She let her mind roam, not dwelling on what might be—that was blasphemous, trying to guess what the future held—but on the journey they'd had and her time with Eodan. They hadn't shared a bed since that first night, though the morning had been spectacular. Though that was likely why they hadn't shared a bed; they were both still too injured for any more robust activities, and it had been hard to remember that while they lay close together, touching and kissing and everything in between.

She brushed her fingers across her grace, wishing she wasn't wearing gloves so she could feel its smooth surface. Eodan was fascinated by it, and she felt she'd seen it anew through his eyes. The thought of losing it terrified her, and yet she was sworn to do her duty. If the Blessed decided Ginnevra's choices made her no longer a paladin, well, she didn't think it was expecting the future to know she would bow to whatever the Blessed chose.

The sound of running footsteps pulled her back to the present. The child ran up to the guards and said, "Ginnevra Cassaline is to come immediately."

Ginnevra wondered how the Blessed knew it was her, given that she'd said nothing that identified her mission or herself. She swallowed against a suddenly tight throat and walked forward. The guards bowed to her and waved her through.

The child, unexpectedly, had waited for her. "I'm to take you to see the Blessed immediately, my lady," she said in her piping voice. Ginnevra still had no idea how old children were based on their sizes, but she didn't think this one could be more than ten. She followed the girl at a trot as the child ran off without asking if Ginnevra was in a hurry. Ginnevra hoped that didn't mean the *Blessed* was in a hurry to see her, but, again, there was nothing she could do if she was.

It took almost no time for them to pass through the gates to the Citadel and then make their way through the narrow, dark passages to the Blessed's chamber. The child opened the door for Ginnevra and said, "This is the paladin, Holy One."

"Enter," the Blessed said. Ginnevra said a quick, fervent prayer even she didn't know the content of and walked through the door.

The room seemed brighter than it had the last time, but Ginnevra didn't know whether there were more lamps than before or those lamps burned brighter. The Blessed sat facing Ginnevra, her hands folded in her lap with her long black sleeves falling over them. Her face was as serene as ever, her eyes as fathomless. "Ginnevra Cassaline," she said. "Please, have a seat."

Ginnevra drew her sword and saluted, then sat, laying the sword carefully on the floor so it didn't make more than a soft rattling sound. She folded her hands in her lap, mimicking the Blessed. "Holy One," she said.

The Blessed leaned back in her seat. "I believe you have something to tell me," she said. "Or, rather, I think you would have returned to your company and not to me if you did not have an extraordinary experience."

"I did, Holy One." Ginnevra squeezed her hands more tightly together to still their shaking. For once, it wasn't nerves, it was anticipation. She found herself eager to tell the Blessed everything, and never mind what it might mean to her personally.

The Blessed nodded slightly, indicating Ginnevra should proceed. Ginnevra drew in a deep breath and let it out slowly. "Holy One, I traveled to Arrus expecting to slay monsters," she said. "But what I found there surpassed all my expectations. Not all the creatures we face are monstrous, Holy One. And..." She drew in another breath. "Let me tell you the story, and I hope you'll understand."

She told the Blessed everything, every private detail, every mistake she'd made. Every moment she'd had with Eodan, including falling in love and her fears of being outcast for that love. The whole grisly ending, with Gasparo's maiming and Damiano's death. And, leaving nothing out, her plea to the Goddess and the Goddess's remarkable response. To her surprise, she found she remembered every word she'd spoken in her prayer. Maybe that, too, was the Goddess's blessing.

When she finished, she felt as cleansed as if someone had scoured her inside and out. She relaxed her hands and waited. The Blessed hadn't moved throughout the story aside from the occasional blink. Now, she unfolded her arms and stood. "I wonder," she said quietly, "what you believe I should do with this extraordinary tale. You admit to sheltering—worse than sheltering—a monster you are sworn to kill, and you admit to sympathy for a legendary creature whose kind have been known to devastate human settlements. What kind of paladin does that make you?"

Ginnevra faced her fearlessly. "The kind who chooses honor over tradition, I hope," she said.

The Blessed arched a single dark eyebrow. "You call your behavior honorable?"

Ginnevra rose and discovered, to her surprise, that the Blessed, while slimmer than she, was of a height with her. "Paladins fight the Bright One's monsters because she hates humanity and everything her Dark Sister stands for. We fight them because they first fought us. If they choose a different path, how is it justice to kill them simply because of who created them? I believe the werewolves, many of them, would like nothing more than to be free of the Bright One and her horrible destinies, and that makes them no different from the humans who turn their backs on her. My honor does not lie in indiscriminate murder. It lies in serving the Dark Lady and what I believe Her wishes to be."

"And the dragon?" the Blessed asked.

Ginnevra remembered how it had felt when the dragon pressed its head against her chest, and unexpected tears welled up. She blinked them away and said, "I felt sorry for it. Maybe that was wrong, because it was dangerous and powerful and it could have killed me—could have killed all of us in that clearing. But it let me touch it, and it looked me in the eye and I think it knew I meant to end its life, and I could think of nothing but how much I wanted a different path." Blinking wasn't working. She cursed herself silently for looking weak in front of the holiest woman in the world and swiped a gloved hand across her eyes.

The Blessed didn't remark on her tears. "And the Goddess granted your plea," she said.

Ginnevra nodded. "I don't know why. I don't think I'm any more deserving of Her grace than anyone else. Maybe it's something only an anointed will understand. But, Holy One—surely it means something that the Goddess was willing to heal a monster! She sees farther than we do, and She knows our hearts—couldn't that extend to the creatures we think are monstrous?"

"Even I don't try to divine the mind of the Dark Lady, Ginnevra." The Blessed sounded tired. She gestured, and the lights dimmed to a more comfortable level, wrapping them both in what reminded Ginnevra of the last light of sunset.

The Blessed resumed her seat, gesturing to Ginnevra to do the same. "I ask again, what do you think I should do with the problem you've handed me?" she said. "You must have some opinion."

It startled Ginnevra so much she let her mouth hang open for a moment, gathering her thoughts. "I don't know what's possible," she said finally. "I thought...I don't know. That maybe we should talk to the werewolves rather than killing them out of hand. It can't be right that they're left without a Goddess simply because they were created by someone who took away their free will. But there are enough of them who still follow the Bright One that I don't think that's safe for us—we can't tell by looking who's who."

"And that is the heart of the problem," the Blessed said. "Paladins fight monsters. They can't afford to stop to question them as to their affiliation."

"Most monsters are still monsters," Ginnevra said. "And paladins still have a duty to protect humans. But the werewolves—"

"I think your loyalties may be suspect," the Blessed said. To Ginnevra's surprise, she was smiling. "Love changes everything."

Ginnevra blushed. "I admit I don't want to give Eodan up. But I don't have a solution for that, either. I can't protect him from every paladin and anointed in the world, and if we stay together, if I am still a paladin, he can't avoid them forever." She ducked her head, not willing to see if the Blessed thought the problem was irrelevant because she was no longer a paladin.

"Hmm," the Blessed said. She stood again. "No, don't get up," she said when Ginnevra shifted to join her. She laid her hands on Ginnevra's bare head and bowed her own. "Dark Lady," she said, "grant us Your wisdom. Your servant Ginnevra has brought me a puzzle. I ask Your blessing upon me to solve it."

Silence filled the room, a silence so great the absence of noise sucked at Ginnevra's ears and made her skin tingle. Then a voice like thunderous silk, a voice that felt as if it came from deep inside Ginnevra's head, said, *She is a witness.*

"A witness to what?" the Blessed said. She sounded not at all awed by the voice's power.

A witness to change. It is time for a new choice.

"Then we were wrong to call all creatures monsters?" the Blessed said.

Do not warp my words, Cristinna. The voice sounded amused rather than rebuking. *You chose well before. You know more now, and you choose again.*

The Blessed's hands shifted slightly on Ginnevra's head, pressing down not quite hard enough to be painful. "And of Ginnevra's inappropriate lover?"

She has the courage to live her convictions, and where courage is, love is never far behind. And I think, when you see him, you will understand better.

Ginnevra blushed even harder at the knowing, amused tone of the Goddess's voice. She wished she dared respond, but this was not a conversation she had any part in.

"Is that a promise for the future?" the Blessed said.

I never show you the future, just the choices that will let you make your own. But I know you well enough to say with certainty that you will not be satisfied until you have spoken with the impossible werewolf. The Goddess sounded even more amused than before.

"I will need to tell Your children something," the Blessed said. "Will You welcome the werewolves who turn their backs on Your Bright Sister?"

There was a pause in which Ginnevra's skin felt stretched nearly to breaking. *I cannot break My word,* the Goddess finally said. *There are rules. There are reasons. If I challenge My Sister, it will be war, and your people would not survive it. But where one change happens, another is possible.*

"I understand, Dark Lady," the Blessed said. "And, as always, I choose to be Your hand."

Blessings upon you, Cristinna. And upon you, Ginnevra. You dared much, and in daring, you opened a door even I thought closed forever. Let your compassion guide you, and your choices will be endless.

Warmth like the summer sun wrapped Ginnevra in its peace, and then the room's silence was merely that of a closed-off chamber, and the voice's echoing presence in Ginnevra's head was gone. The Blessed removed her hands from Ginnevra's head with a sigh and returned to her seat. "Well," she said, "I suppose I should have expected no less from the divine inscrutability."

"I don't understand what She meant," Ginnevra said. "She can't accept the werewolves because of Her word?"

"More to the point, She would like to break Her word, but will not for our sake." The Blessed sighed again and tilted her head back, a casual gesture that stunned Ginnevra. "Which is probably for the best. What you've learned will be hard for even the anointed to accept, and harder still for the paladins who have fought werewolves. But where the Blessed gives us opportunities, it's our honor to choose to accept them."

"I'm still not sure I understand. I'm not a theologian."

"No, and for that I am grateful," the Blessed said cryptically. "Tomorrow, I will meet with you and Eodan in the inner city. I'll send word with the time and location. I'm sorry, but there's no way I can permit a werewolf, monster or no, into the Citadel."

"Of course. I understand."

"Good. I want to speak with him about his people and about what they want. What we can do for them." The Blessed turned her chair around to face her desk and picked up a pen. "And I want you to write your experience for the Citadel's records, exactly as you told me. You shouldn't be expected to repeat yourself a million times, and everyone will want to know the details."

Ginnevra's heart sank. Paladins had to be literate, but she wasn't much of a scholar and had terrible penmanship. "I'm afraid I'm not good at writing," she said.

"Don't worry about that. Do you have any other questions?"

"No—I mean, yes. When can I rejoin my company?"

The Blessed turned in her seat and fixed Ginnevra with her fathomless black eyes. "I don't think you should," she said.

It hit Ginnevra like a knife to the chest. She controlled her reaction and said, "If that's what you require, I will obey," and reached behind her neck to fumble with the clasp of her grace.

"Oh, I didn't mean that," the Blessed said. "You and I both realize the difficulties you face, being romantically involved with a werewolf. I wouldn't tell you to give him up even if I didn't have a strong suspicion the Goddess is in favor of your union. She has the oddest sense of humor sometimes. And yet I can't quite picture a werewolf living quietly in our cities, waiting on your return from your missions. No, on the whole I think it's better if you are separated from a company. I'm sorry, because I'm sure you're attached to them, but it seems the best solution."

Ginnevra found she still couldn't breathe properly. "I don't understand," she said, then felt stupid at how often she'd said this to her religious superior. "What will I do instead?"

"The same thing you did at Arrus, probably," the Blessed said. "There are a few paladins who are unsuited to life within a company, for various reasons. As I occasionally have tasks that require more subtlety than a company can manage, those paladins, my primes, serve me well." She smiled. "A paladin together with a werewolf...the possibilities are intriguing."

To serve as one of the Blessed's primes. It wasn't anything Ginnevra had ever dreamed of for herself. She couldn't begin to imagine what else she might do, but she was tired of sounding like an ignorant fool. "It will be my honor to serve," she said.

The Blessed nodded. "You have my leave to depart," she said, once more sounding formal. "I will see you and Eodan tomorrow. And I honor you for having the courage to do something very few women would ever have thought to do."

Ginnevra saluted her again and let herself out.

The message runner had disappeared, and Ginnevra made a few wrong turns before reaching the courtyard. This time, a company of paladins crossed the paving stones, headed for the sanctification hall entrance. She waited for them to pass before crossing the courtyard to the gate. Her heart ached a little at the knowledge that she was unlikely to enjoy the close sisterhood of a company again, but only a little. What the Blessed wanted of her was an adventure like no other, and she couldn't stay sad when she contemplated it.

As she walked, she became aware of something strange pressing against her wounded side. Halfway through the Bastion, she stopped and wiggled her fingers under her shirt, gambeson, and cuirass. She pulled the bandage free and prodded her side, which still felt strange. More fierce prodding revealed that her wound was gone. Ginnevra closed her eyes and touched her grace. "It's more than I deserve," she whispered, "but I hope You know I would serve You regardless." It felt like a blessing on her new life, and the last of her sadness fell away.

Her excitement grew as she passed through the city until she had to stop herself from skipping through the outer city to the inn. She gave the innkeeper a cheery wave and was halfway down the hall when she realized he was calling to her. "My lady," he said as he trotted to catch up, "the room...I discovered it needed...it was unsuitable, and I moved you and your companion elsewhere."

His attempt to cover his mistake without claiming his inn had rats or some other vermin amused Ginnevra, but she kept from laughing out of politeness. "Will you show me there?" she asked.

The new room was on an upper floor, on a corner with big glass windows that let in as much sunlight as the thick clouds permitted. There were still two beds, but they were wider than the first and had thicker mattresses. Eodan lay on one of the beds, snoring, but he came awake when the door opened. "Thank you," Ginnevra said to the innkeeper, and meant it. Maybe he was pandering, but she wouldn't turn down a generous offer out of suspicion of someone's motives.

"You still have your grace," Eodan said as Ginnevra began removing her armor. "I take it that's a good sign."

"Nothing happened as I expected, which ought to be a reminder to me not to anticipate a given future." Ginnevra set each piece of armor in a pile in the corner, well away from where Eodan sat.

"Then what did happen?"

Ginnevra stripped off her vambraces and pulled her gambeson off over her head. "So much. I don't know where to begin. But—" She sat beside him and put her arm around his waist. "What matters is we're together, and we're going to stay that way."

Eodan's eyebrows raised. "We are?"

"Don't sound so surprised. It's what you wanted." Ginnevra kissed him, her lips lingering on his, and put her other arm around his neck.

"Of course, but I thought it was impossible." He kissed her in return, his hand resting on her thigh.

"Not impossible. Not even unlikely. And the Goddess thinks you're handsome."

Eodan's head jerked back. "What?"

Ginnevra laughed. "It's not important. What's important is that I'm fully healed, we have a lovely room, and no one's demanding our time." She slipped her hands beneath his shirt, which had dried stiff from the rainwater, and worked at the laces tying his breeches.

Eodan captured her hands in one of his large ones. "You're going to have to explain more than that. You're healed? Is that something the Blessed can do?"

"I don't know." Ginnevra felt dizzy with joy and relief. "There's so much to tell, but right now all I know is that I love you, and I want more than anything to share that love. Everything else can wait." She kissed him again, freeing her hand from his loose grasp to caress his cheek.

He put his arms around her, pulling her close in the tender gesture that never failed to make her heart race. "Goddess forbid I argue with that," he said, and kissed her in return.

About the Author

In addition to the Books of the Dark Goddess, Melissa McShane is the author of many other fantasy novels, including the novels of Tremontane, the first of which is *Servant of the Crown; Burning Bright,* first in The Extraordinaries series; and *The Book of Secrets,* first book in The Last Oracle series.

She lives in the shelter of the mountains out West with her family, including two very needy cats. She wrote reviews and critical essays for many years before turning to fiction, which is much more fun than anyone ought to be allowed to have. You can visit her at her website **www.melissamcshanewrites.com** for more information on other books and upcoming releases.

For news on upcoming releases, bonus material, and other fun stuff, sign up for Melissa's newsletter **here**.

ALSO BY MELISSA MCSHANE

THE LIVING ORACLE

Hidden Realm (forthcoming)

THE NOVELS OF TREMONTANE

Pretender to the Crown

Guardian of the Crown

Champion of the Crown

Ally of the Crown

Stranger to the Crown

Scholar of the Crown

Servant of the Crown

Exile of the Crown

Rider of the Crown

Agent of the Crown

Voyager of the Crown

Tales of the Crown

COMPANY OF STRANGERS

Company of Strangers

Stone of Inheritance

Mortal Rites

Shifting Loyalties

Sands of Memory

Call of Wizardry

THE DRAGONS OF MOTHER STONE

Spark the Fire

Faith in Flames

Ember in Shadow

Made in the USA
Coppell, TX
18 May 2024

32503531R00115